# DEADLY HONEYMOON

# *DEADLY*
# HONEYMOON

## *by Lawrence Block*

Carroll & Graf Publishers, Inc.
New York

First Carroll & Graf edition 1995

Carroll & Graf Publishers, Inc.
260 Fifth Avenue
New York, NY 10001

ISBN 0-7867-0226-5

Manufactured in the United States of America

For *Don Westlake*

# DEADLY HONEYMOON

# 1

Just EAST OF the Binghamton city limits he pulled the car off the road and cut the motor. She leaned toward him and he kissed her. He said, "Good morning, Mrs. Wade."

"Mmmm," she said. "I think I like my new name. What are we stopping for, honey?"

"I ran out of gas." He kissed her again. "No, they gimmicked the car. Shoes and everything. You didn't notice?"

"No."

He got out of the car and walked around the back. Four old shoes trailed from the license-plate mounting. On the lid of the trunk someone had painted JUST MARRIED in four-inch white letters. He got down on one knee and picked at the knots in the shoelaces. They were tight. The car door opened on her side and she got out and came back to watch him.

When he looked up at her she was starting to laugh softly.

"I didn't even notice it," she said. "Too busy ducking rice. I'm glad we got married in church. Dave, imagine driving all through Pennsylvania with the car like that! It's good you noticed."

"Uh-huh. You don't have a knife handy, do you?"

"To defend my honor? No. Let me get it. I have long fingernails."

"Never mind." He straightened up, the shoes in hand. He grinned at her. "Those crazy guys," he said. "What are we supposed to do with these?"

"I don't know."

"I mean, is it good luck to keep them?"

"If the shoe fits—"

He laughed happily and tossed the shoes into the underbrush at the side of the road. He unlocked the trunk, hauled out a rag, and wiped at the paint on the trunk lid. It wouldn't come off. There was an extra can of gasoline in the trunk, and he uncapped it and soaked the rag with gas. This time the paint came off easily. He wiped the trunk lid dry with a clean rag to protect the car's finish, then tossed both rags off to the side of the road and slammed the trunk shut.

She said, "I didn't know you were a litterbug."

"You can't carry them in the trunk, not soaked with gas. They could start a fire."

"That's grounds for an annulment, you know."

"Starting a fire?"

"Concealing the fact that you're a litterbug."

"Want an annulment?"

"God, no," she said.

She had changed from her wedding dress to a lime-green

sheath that was snug on her big body. Her hair was blond, shoulder length, worn pageboy style with the ends curled under. Her eyes were large, and just a shade deeper in color than the dress. He looked at her and thought how very beautiful she was. He took a step toward her, not even conscious of his own movement.

"Dave, we'd better get going."

"Mmmm."

"We've got three weeks. We waited this long, we can wait two more hours. And this is an awfully public place, isn't it?"

Her tone was not quite as light as her words. He turned from her. Cars passed them on the highway. He grinned suddenly and got back into the car. She got in on her side and sat next to him, close to him. He turned the key in the ignition and started the car and pulled back onto the road.

From Binghamton they rode south on 81, the new Penn-Can Highway. Jill had a state map spread open on her lap and she studied it from time to time but it was hardly necessary. He just kept the car on the road and held the speed steady between sixty and sixty-five. The car was a middleweight Ford, the Fairlane, last year's model. It was the second week in September now and the car had a shade less than fifteen thousand miles on it.

They crossed the Pennsylvania state line a few minutes after noon. At twelve-thirty they left Route 81 at a town called Lenox and cut southeast on 106 through Carbondale and Honesdale. The new road was narrower, a two-laner that zigzagged across the hills. They pulled into an Esso station in Honesdale and Jill had a chicken sandwich at a

diner two doors down from the station. He had a Coke and
left half of it.

A few miles further on, at Indian Orchard, they left 106
and continued south on U.S. 6. They were at Pomquit by a
quarter to two. Pomquit was at the northern tip of Lake Wallenpaupack, and their lodge was on the western rim of the
lake, half a dozen miles south of the town. They found it
without stopping for directions. The lodge had a private
road. They followed its curves through a thick stand of white
pine and parked in front of a large white Victorian house
bounded on three sides by a huge porch. They could see the
lake from where the car was parked. The water was very
still, very blue.

Inside, in the office, a gray-haired woman sat behind a
desk drinking whiskey and water. She looked up at them,
and Dave told her his name. The woman shuffled through
a stack of four-by-six file cards and found their reservation.

"Wade, David. You wanted a cabin, is that right?"

"That's right."

"Honeymooners, I guess, and I don't blame you. Wanting
a cabin, that is. Rooms in the lodge are nice but you don't
get the privacy here you would be getting in a cabin. It's an
old house. Sounds carry. And privacy is important, God
knows. On a honeymoon."

Jill was not blushing. The woman said, "You picked a good
time of the year now. What with the lake and the mountains
it stays pretty cool here most of the time, but this year July
and August got pretty hot, pretty hot. And on a honeymoon
you don't want it to be too warm. But it's cooled off
now."

She passed the card to him. On a dotted line across the

bottom he wrote, "Mr. and Mrs. David Wade," writing the double signature with an odd combination of pride and embarrassment. The woman filed the card away without looking at it. She gave him a key and offered halfheartedly to show them where the cabin was. He said he thought they could find it themselves. She told him how to get there, what path to take. They went back to the car and drove along a one-lane path that skirted the edge of the lake. Their cabin was the fourth one down. He parked the Ford alongside the cabin and got out of the car.

Their suitcases—two pieces, matching, a gift from an aunt and uncle of his—were in the back seat. He carried them up onto the cabin's small porch, set them down, unlocked the door, carried them inside. She waited outside, and he came back for her and grinned at her.

"I'm waiting," she said.

He lifted her easily and carried her over the threshold, crossed the room, set her down gently on the edge of the double bed. "I should have married a little girl," he said.

"You like little girls?"

"I like big blondes the best. But little girls are easier to carry."

"Oh, they are?"

"It seems likely, doesn't it?"

"Ever carry any?"

"Never."

"Liar," she said. Then, "That drunken old woman has a dirty mind."

"She wasn't drunk, just drinking. And her mind's not dirty."

"What is it?"

"Realistic."

"Lecher."

"Uh-huh."

He looked at her, sitting on the edge of the bed, their bed. She was twenty-four, two years younger than he was, and no man had ever made love to her. He was surprised how glad he was of this. Before they met he had always felt that it wouldn't matter to him what any woman of his had done with other men before their marriage, but now he knew that he had been wrong, that he did care, that he was glad no one had ever possessed her. And that they had waited. Their first time would be now, here, together, and after the wedding.

He sat down next to her. She turned toward him and he kissed her, and she made a purring sound and came up close against him. He felt the sweet and certain pressure of her body against his.

Now, if he wanted it. But it was the middle of the afternoon and sunlight streamed through the cabin windows. The first time should be just right, he thought. At night, under a blanket of darkness.

He kissed her once more, then stood up and crossed the small room to look out through the window. "The lake's beautiful," he said easily. "Want to swim a little?"

"I love you," she said.

He drew the shades. Then he went outside and closed the door to wait on the porch while she changed into her bathing suit. He smoked a cigarette and looked out at the lake.

He was twenty-six, two years out of law school. In a year or so he would be a junior partner in his father's firm. He was married. He loved his wife.

A heavyset man waved to him from the steps of the cabin next door. He waved back. It was a good day, he thought. It would be a good three weeks.

Jill was a better swimmer than he was. He spent most of his time standing in cool water up to his waist, watching the perfect synchronization of her body. Her blond hair was all bunched up under her white bathing cap.

Later she came over to him and he kissed her. "Let's go sit under a tree or something," she said. "I don't want to get a burn."

"Jesus, no," he said. "Sunburned on your honeymoon—"

"You sound like that drunken old woman."

He spread a blanket on the bank and they sat together and shared a cigarette. Their shoulders were just touching. There were small woodland noises as a background, and once in a while the faraway sound of a car on the highway. That was all. He dried her back and shoulders with a towel and she took off her bathing cap and let her hair spill down.

Around five the man from the cabin next door, the one who had waved, came over to them carrying three cans of Budweiser. He said, "You kids just moved in. I thought maybe you'd have a beer with me."

He was between forty-five and fifty, maybe thirty pounds overweight. He wore a pair of gray gabardine slacks and a navy-blue open-necked sport shirt. His forearms were brown from the sun. He had a round face, the skin ruddy under his deep tan.

They thanked him, asked him to sit down. They each took a can of beer. It was very cold and very good. The man sat down on the edge of their blanket and told them that his name was Joe Carroll and that he was from New York. Dave introduced himself and Jill and said that they were from Binghamton. Carroll said he had never been to Binghamton. He took a long drink of beer and wiped his mouth with the back of his hand. He asked them if they were staying long.

"Three weeks," Dave said.

"You picked a good spot. We been having good weather, cooler now than it was, with sun just about every day. A little rain the week before last, but not too much."

"Have you been here long, Mr. Carroll?" Jill asked.

"Joe. Yeah, most of the summer. I'm just here by myself. You can go crazy for somebody to talk to. You kids been married long?"

"Not too long," Dave said.

"Any kids?"

"Not yet."

Carroll looked off at the lake. "I never got married. Almost, once, but I didn't. I'll tell you the truth, I never missed it. Except for kids. Sometimes I miss not having kids." He finished his beer, held the can in one hand and looked at it. "But what with business and all, you know, a man stays pretty busy."

"You're in business."

"Construction." He waved a hand in the general direction of the lake. "Out on Long Island, Nassau County, the developments. We built, oh, a whole lot of those houses."

"Isn't this your busy season?"

He laughed shortly. "Oh, I'm out of it now, for the time being."

"Retired?"

"You could call it that." Carroll smiled as if at a private joke. "I may relocate," he said. "I might pull up stakes, find a better territory."

They made small talk. Baseball, the weather, the woman who managed the lodge. Carroll said she was a widow, childless. Her husband had died five or six years back, and she was running the place on her own and making a fairly good thing of it. He said she was a minor-league alcoholic, never blind drunk but never quite sober. "The hell," he said, "what else has she got, huh?"

He told them about a steak house down the road where the food wasn't bad. "Listen," he said, "you get a chance, drop over to my place. We'll sit around a little."

"Well—"

"There's more beer, I got a hot plate for coffee. You know gin rummy? We could play a few hands and pass the time."

They ate at the steak house that Carroll recommended. It was just outside of Pomquit. The steaks were thick, the service fast, and the place had the atmosphere of a Colonial tavern, authentic without being intrusive. There was an old copper kettle hanging from a hook on one wall, and Jill wanted it. Dave tried to buy it but the manager said it wasn't for sale. They stood outside for a few minutes after dinner and looked up at the moon. It was just a little less than full.

"Honeymoon," she said. "Keep a-shining in June. But it's September, isn't it?"

"The drunken old woman said it's better this way. You don't want it too hot on a honeymoon."

"Oh, no?"

"Now who's the lecher?"

"I'm shameless," she said. "Let's go back to the cabin. I think I love you, Mr. Wade."

On the slow ride home she said, "I feel sorry for him."

"Who, Carroll?"

"Yes. He's so lonely it's sad. Why would he pick a spot like this to come to all alone?"

"Well, he said the fishing—"

"But all alone? There are livelier spots where the fishing must be just as good as it is here."

"Listen, he just sold his business. Maybe he's got problems."

"He should have gotten married," she said. She rolled down her window, let her arm hang out, tapped against the side of the Ford with her long fingernails. "Everybody should be married. Maybe he'll marry the drunken old woman and she won't drink any more and they can manage the lodge together."

"Or tear it down and build up a tract of ugly little split-levels."

"Either way," she said. "Everybody should be married. Married is fun."

"You're incorrigible," he said.

"I love you."

He almost missed the turnoff for the lodge. He cut the wheel sharply to the left and the Ford moved onto the private road. He drove past the lodge itself and followed the path back to the cabin. The lights were on in Joe Carroll's cabin. She said, "Mr. Carroll wanted us to stop in for coffee."

"Some other time," he said.

He parked the car and they walked slowly together up the

steps to the cabin. He unlocked the door, turned on the light. They went inside and he closed the door and turned the bolt. She looked at him and he kissed her and she said, "Oh, God." He turned off the light. The room was not completely dark. A little light came in, from the moon on one side, from Carroll's cabin on the other.

He held her and she threw her arms around his neck and kissed him. She was a tall girl, a soft and warm girl. His. He found the zipper of her dress and opened it partway and rubbed her back with his fingers.

Outside, a car drew up slowly. The motor died and the car coasted to a stop.

She stiffened. "There's somebody coming," she said.

"Not here."

"I heard a car—"

"Probably some friends of Carroll's."

"I hope it's not some friends of ours," she said, her voice almost savage. "I hope this isn't some idiot's idea of a joke."

"They wouldn't do that."

"I just hope not."

He let go of her. "Maybe I'd better check," he said.

The bolt on the door was stuck. He wrestled it open, turned the doorknob, opened the door, and stepped outside onto the porch. Jill followed him, stood at his side. The car, empty now, was parked in front of their cabin by the side of the Ford. It was a big car, a Buick or an Olds. It was dark, and he couldn't be sure of the color in the half-light. Maybe black, maybe maroon or dark green. The two men who had been in the car were walking toward Carroll's cabin. They were short men and they wore hats and dark suits.

He turned to her. "See? Friends of Joe's."

"Then why didn't they park at his cabin?" He looked at her. "They drove right past his cabin," she said, "and they parked here, and now they're walking back. Why?"

"What's the difference?"

He took her arm and started to lead her inside again. But she shrugged and stayed where she was. "Just a minute," she said.

"What's the matter?"

"I don't know. Wait a minute, Dave."

They waited and watched. Carroll's cabin was thirty or forty yards from theirs. The men covered the distance without making any noise. One of Carroll's porch steps creaked, and just after the creak they could hear movement inside the cabin. The men did not knock. One of them yanked the door open and the other sprang inside. The man on the porch had something in his hand, something that light glinted off, as though it were metallic.

Sounds came from the cabin, sounds that were hard to make out. Then Joe Carroll walked out of the cabin and the man who had remained outside said something to him in a low voice. They could see what he had in his hand now. It was a gun. The other man came out behind Carroll and he was holding a gun in Carroll's back.

They stayed on the porch and they stayed quiet. It wasn't real—that was all he could think, that it was not real, that it was a play or a movie and not something happening before them.

They heard Carroll's voice, crystal clear in the still night air. "I'll make it good," he said. "I swear to God I'll make it good. You tell Lublin I'll make it good, Jesus, just tell him."

The man behind him, the one jabbing him in the back

with the gun, began to laugh quietly. It was unpleasant laughter.

"Oh, sweet Jesus," Carroll said. His face was awful. "Listen, please, just a chance, just give me a chance—"

"Crawl," the man in front said.

"What do you want me to—"

"Get down on your knees and beg, you bastard."

Carroll sank to his knees. There were fallen leaves on the ground, and pine needles. He was saying something over and over again in a weak voice but they couldn't quite make it out.

The man in front stepped forward and put the muzzle of his gun against Carroll's head. Carroll started to whine. The man shot him in the center of the forehead and he shook from the blow and pitched forward on his face. The other man moved in and shot Carroll four times through the back of his head.

Jill screamed.

It wasn't much of a scream. It broke off in no time at all, and it was neither very loud nor very high-pitched. But the two men in the dark suits heard it. They heard it and they looked up at the porch of the Wade cabin.

And came forward.

They stood, the four of them, in Carroll's cabin. The small room was as neat as if no one had ever lived in it. There was a hot plate on an oak table, with a large jar of Yuban instant coffee beside it and a half-finished cup of coffee off to one side. The bed was neatly made.

The taller of the two men was called Lee. They knew this, but they did not know whether it was his first name or his

21

last name. He was the one who had made Carroll crawl, the one who had killed him with the first shot in the forehead. Lee had large brown eyes and thick black eyebrows. There were three or four thin scars across the bridge of his nose. His mouth was a thin line, the lips pale. He was holding a gun on them now while the other man, whose name they had not heard yet, was systematically going through Carroll's dresser drawers, taking everything out piece by piece, throwing everything on the floor.

"Nothing," he said finally. "Just what was in the wallet."

Lee didn't say anything. The shorter man turned around and nodded toward Dave and Jill. He was heavier than Lee, with a thick neck and a nose that had been broken and imperfectly reset. He looked as though he might have played guard or tackle on some college's junior varsity.

Now he said, "What about them?"

"They didn't see a thing. They aren't going to talk."

"What if they do?"

"So? They don't know a thing."

"We won't make any trouble," Dave said. His voice sounded odd to him, as though someone else were pulling strings that moved his lips, as though someone else were talking for him.

They didn't seem to have heard him. Lee said, "If they talk, it doesn't matter. They talk to some hick cop and he writes it all down and everybody forgets it. They put it in some drawer."

"We could make sure."

"Just let us alone," Dave said. Jill was next to him, breathing heavily. He looked at the gun in Lee's hand and won-

22

dered whether they were going to die, now, in this cabin. "Just let us live," he said.

"We kill 'em," Lee said, "it makes too much stink. Him out there, that's one thing, but you kill a couple of kids—"

"Leave 'em alone then?"

"Yeah."

"Just like that?"

"I don't like killing nobody without I get paid for it," Lee said. "I don't like throwing any in for free."

The man with the broken nose nodded. He said, "The broad."

"What about her?"

"She's nice. Stacked."

Dave said, "Now listen—"

They ignored him. "You want her?"

"Why not?"

The man called Lee smiled brutally. He stepped up to Jill and stuck the gun into her chest just below and between her breasts. "How about that," he said. "You don't mind a little screwing just to keep you alive, now, do you?"

Dave stepped out and swung at him. He threw a left, hard, not thinking, just reacting. The man called Lee stepped back and let the punch go over his shoulder. He reversed the gun in his hand and laid the side of the gun butt across Dave's forehead. Dave took one more little step, a half-step, really, and fell to the floor.

His head was spinning. He got to one knee. The shorter man was pushing Jill toward Carroll's bed. She was crying hysterically but was not fighting very hard. There was the sound of cloth ripping, Jill's shrill scream above the tearing of the dress. He pushed himself up and rushed toward the bed, and Lee stuck out a foot and tripped him. He went sprawling. Lee stepped in close and kicked him in the side of the rib cage. He moaned and fell flat on his face.

"You better take it easy," Lee said.

He got up again. He stood, wavering, and Lee set the gun down on the table. He moved as if he had all the time in the world. Dave stood there, staring dead ahead, and Lee moved in front of him and hit him in the pit of the stomach. He doubled over but he didn't go down. Lee waited, and he straightened up, and Lee hit him twice in the chest and once in the stomach. This time he went down again. He tried to get up but he couldn't. It was as though someone had cut all his tendons. He was awake, he knew what was happening, he just couldn't move.

Jill had stopped crying. The shorter man finished with her and came over to them. He asked Lee whether Dave had tried to be a hero. Lee didn't say anything. Then the shorter man said, "She was cherry. You believe that?" And he said it as though he had not known virgins still existed.

Lee said, "She ain't now." And took off his jacket and went to take the shorter man's place with Jill.

She didn't scream. She lay there, motionless, and Dave thought that they must have killed her. This time his legs worked, this time he got up. The shorter man hit him with the gun and pain split his skull in half. He went down. The world turned gray, and the gray darkened quickly to black.

# 2

◄◄◄◄◄◄◄◄◄◄◄◄◄◄◄◄◄◄◄◄◄◄◄◄◄◄◄◄◄◄◄◄◄◄◄◄◄◄◄◄◄◄◄◄◄

HE NEVER REMEMBERED going back to the cabin. He had vague memories of walking and falling down, walking and falling down, but they were as dim as vanished dreams. When he did come out of it, he was in their own cabin. He was lying on the bed and Jill was sitting in a chair looking down at him. She was wearing a beige skirt and a dark-brown sweater. Her face was freshly scrubbed, her lipstick unmarred, her hair neatly combed. There was a moment, then, when nothing made sense—the whole thing, Carroll and the two men and the beating and the violation of his wife, none of this could have happened.

But then he felt the pain in his own body and the dull ache of his head and he saw the discoloration over her right eye, masked incompletely by makeup. It had all happened.

"Don't try to talk yet," she said. "Take it easy."

"I'm all right."

"Dave—"

"I'm all right," he said. He sat up. His head was perfectly clear now. The pain was still there, and strong, but his head was perfectly clear. He remembered everything up to the blow that knocked him out. The return from Carroll's cabin to their own, that was lost, but he remembered all the rest in awful reality.

"We've got to get you to a doctor," he said.

"I'm all right."

"Did they—"

"Yes."

"Both of them?"

"Both of them."

"You've got to see a doctor, Jill."

"Tomorrow, then." She took a breath. "I think the police are over in . . . in the other cabin. I heard a car, someone must have called them. It took them long enough."

"What time is it?"

"After ten. They'll be coming over here, won't they?"

"The police? Yes, I think so."

"You'd better clean up. I tried to wash your face. Your head is cut a little. In two places, on top and behind your ear there." She touched him, her hand light, cool. "How do you feel?"

"All right."

"Liar," she said. "Wash up and change your clothes, Dave."

He went into the tiny bathroom and stripped down. There

was no tub, just a shower. It was one of those showers in which you had to hold a chain down in order to keep the water running. He showered very quickly and thought about the two men and Carroll and about what they had done to Jill. At first his mind clouded with fury, but he stayed in the shower and the water rained down upon him, and he thought about it, forced himself to think about it. The fury did not go away. It stayed, but it cooled and changed its shape.

While he was drying himself off the bathroom door opened and Jill brought him clean clothes. After she had left he realized, oddly, that she had just seen him naked for the first time. He shrugged the thought away and dressed.

When he came out of the bathroom, the police were there. There were two tall thin men, state troopers, and there was one older man from the Sheriff's Office in Pomquit. One of the troopers took their names. Then he removed his hat and said, "A man was murdered here tonight, Mr. Wade. We wondered if you knew anything about it."

"Murdered?"

"Your neighbor. A Mr. Carroll."

Jill drew in her breath sharply. Dave looked at her, then at the trooper. "We met Mr. Carroll just this afternoon," he said. "What . . . happened?"

"He was shot four times in the head."

Five times, he thought. He said, "Who did it?"

"We don't know. Did you hear anything? See anything?"

"No."

"Whoever killed him must have come in a car, Mr. Wade. We found tire tracks. There was a car parked right next to yours outside. That is your car, isn't it? The Ford?"

"Yes."

"Did you hear a car drive up, Mr. Wade?"

"Not that I remember."

The man from the Sheriff's Office said, "You would have heard it—it was right outside your window. And the shots, you would have heard them. Were you here all night?"

Jill said, "We went out for dinner."

"What time?"

"We left about seven," she said. "Seven or seven-thirty."

"And got back when?"

"About . . . oh, half an hour ago, I guess. Why?"

The man from the Sheriff's Office looked over at the troopers. "That would do it, then," he said. "Carroll's been dead at least an hour, the way my man figures it. Closer to two hours, probably. They must have gotten back just before we got the call, must have come right in without seeing the body. You wouldn't see it from where the car's parked, anyway. Just been back half an hour, Mr. Wade?"

"It may have been longer than that," he said.

"As much as an hour?"

"I don't think so. Maybe forty-five minutes at the outside."

"That would do it, then. I guess you didn't see anything, then, Mr. Wade. Mrs. Wade."

He turned to go. The troopers hesitated, as though they wanted to say something but hadn't figured out the phrasing yet. Dave said, "Why was he killed?"

"We don't know yet, Mr. Wade."

"He was a very pleasant man. Quiet, friendly. We sat outside this afternoon and had a beer with him."

The troopers didn't say anything.

"Well," Dave said, "I don't want to keep you."

The troopers nodded shortly. They turned, then, and followed the man from the Sheriff's Office out of the cabin.

It was midnight when the last carful of police was gone. They sat quietly for five or ten minutes. He stood up then and said, "We're getting out of here tonight. You'd better start packing."

"We're leaving tonight?"

"You don't want to stay here, do you?"

"God, no." She reached out a hand. He gave her a cigarette, lit it for her. She blew out smoke and said, "They won't be suspicious?"

"Of what?"

"Of us, if we leave so quickly. Without staying the night."

He shook his head. "We're newlyweds," he said. "Newlyweds wouldn't want to spend their wedding night next door to a murder."

"Newlyweds."

"Yes."

"Wedding night. God, Dave, how I planned this night. All of it."

He took her hand.

"How I would be sexy for you and everything. How I wouldn't mind if it hurt because I love you so much. Oh, and little tricks I read in one of those marriage manuals, I was going to try those tricks. And surprise you with my ingenuity."

"Stop it."

He got the suitcases and spread them open on the bed. They packed their clothes in silence. He put the clothes she had worn earlier and his own dirty clothes in the trunk and loaded the two suitcases in the back seat. She got in the car, and he went to the cabin and closed the door and locked it.

As they drove past the lodge, she said, "We didn't pay. The old woman would want to be paid, for the one night."

"That's too fucking bad," he said.

He turned left at the main road and drove to Pomquit. He passed through the town and took a road heading north. "It's late and I don't know the roads," he said. "We'll stop at the first motel that looks decent."

"All right."

"We'll get an early start in the morning," he went on. He was looking straight ahead at the road and he did not glance over at her. "An early start in the morning, figure out which route to take, all of that. They're from New York, aren't they?"

"I think so. Carroll said he was from New York. And they all had New York accents."

He slowed the car. There was a motel off to the left, but the "No Vacancy" sign was lit. He speeded up again.

"We'll go to New York," he said. "We'll be there by tomorrow afternoon, Monday. We'll get a room in a hotel, and we'll find out who they are, the two of them. One of them is named Lee. I didn't catch the other one's name."

"Neither did I."

"We'll find out who they are, and then we'll find them and we'll kill them, both of them. Then we'll go back to Binghamton. We have three weeks. I think we can find them and kill them in three weeks."

Up ahead, on the right, there was a motel. He slowed the car. As he pulled off the road he glanced at her face, quickly. Her jaw was set and her eyes were dry and clear.

"Three weeks is plenty of time," she said.

# 3

<<<<<<<<<<<<<<<<<<<<<<<<<<<<<<<<<<<<<<<<<<<<<<

IN THE DINER the waitress said, "Mondays, how I hate 'em. Give me any other day, but Monday, just never mind. Coffee?"

"One black, one regular," he told her.

There were two men at the counter who looked like truckers and one who looked like a farmer. The waitress brought the coffee and he carried the two cups over to a table on the side. Some of the coffee in her cup spilled out onto the saucer. He took a napkin from the dispenser and wiped up the coffee. She added sugar, one level spoonful. He drank his straight black.

When the waitress came over he ordered toast and a side order of link sausages. Jill wanted a toasted English muffin, but the diner didn't have any. The waitress said there would be some coming in around nine-thirty. Jill had a cheese Danish instead and managed to eat half of it.

He spread a road map on the table and studied it, marking a route with a pencil. She sipped her coffee and looked across the room while he traced the route they would take. By the time he was finished, she had drunk her coffee. He looked up and said, "This is how we'll do it. We're on 590 now. We take it to Ford—that's just across the state line—and pick up 97. We go about five miles on 97 to Route 55. That's at Barryville. Then 55 runs just about due north to something called White Lake, where we get 17B. Then we hook up with 17 at Monticello. That carries us all the way to the throughway at Exit 16, and then we just drive down into New York."

"I never heard of those towns," she said.

"Well, Monticello you've heard of."

"I mean the others."

He sipped his coffee, checked his watch with the electric clock over the counter. "Twenty to eight," he said.

"Should we get going?"

"Pretty soon." He got to his feet. "I'm having another cup of coffee," he said. "How about you?"

"All right."

He carried the two cups back to the counter. The waitress was busy telling one of the truckers what a terrible day Monday was. She was a heavyish woman with stringy hair. When she finished talking to the truck driver Dave got two fresh cups of coffee and carried them back to the table.

They passed through the town, a small one, and a sign told them to resume their normal speed. He bore down on the accelerator. The sun was bright on the road ahead. The sky had been overcast when they got up, but the clouds were mostly gone now.

"That was Forestine," she said. "White Lake in three miles."

"And then what?"

"Then right on 17B."

He nodded. So far, in close to an hour of driving, they had talked only about the route and the road conditions. She had the road map open on her lap, the map with their route penciled in, and she told him when to slow down and where to turn. But most of the time passed in long silences. It was not for lack of things to say to each other, or because any distance had sprung up between them. Small talk did not fit and larger talk came hard.

The night before they had stayed at a motel called Hillcrest Manor. They slept in a double bed. After he checked in, they left their suitcases in the locked car and went inside. They undressed with the lights on, then he turned off the lights, and they got into the large bed. She took the side near the windows, and he had the side nearer to the door. He waited, and she came to him and kissed him once, on the side of the face. Then she went back to her side of the bed. He asked her if she thought she would be able to sleep and she said yes, she thought so. After about fifteen minutes he heard her easy rhythmic breathing and knew that she was sleeping.

He couldn't fall asleep. The beating had tired him, and his body wanted sleep, but it didn't work. He would manage to relax and would start drifting off and then the memory would come, racing in at his mind, and he would suck in breath and shake his head and sit up in the bed, his heart

33

beating fast and hard. From time to time he got out of the bed and sat in a chair at the window, smoking a cigarette in the darkness, then putting out the cigarette and returning to bed.

Around four, he dozed off. At a quarter to six he heard a frightened yelp and was instantly awake. She lay on her back, her head on a pillow, her eyes closed, and she was crying in her sleep. He woke her up and soothed her and told her that everything was all right. After a few minutes she fell asleep again, and he got up and put clothes on.

Now he talked to her without looking at her, his eyes conveniently fixed on the road ahead. "When we get to Monticello," he said, "you're going to see a doctor."

"No."

"Why not?"

He looked at her. She was worrying her lip with her teeth. "I don't want anyone, oh, touching me. Now. Examining me."

"Is that all?"

"I just don't want it. And if a doctor could tell anything, wouldn't he have to report it? Like a gunshot wound?"

"I don't know. But if they injured you—"

"They didn't hurt me," she said. "I mean, they didn't do any damage. I checked, I know. There were no cuts or bleeding." Her voice, flat until then, came alive again. "Dave, those policemen were stupid."

"Why?"

"They figured it all out. The mess in Carroll's cabin, the way everything was turned upside down. They think Carroll fought with his murderers and then they dragged him outside and shot him."

34

"I didn't even think about that. That's what they figure?"

"They were talking outside, before you got out of the shower. Dave, they didn't hurt me. I don't have to see any doctor."

"Well—"

"There wasn't even that much pain," she said. "The doctor I saw, before we were married—"

He waited.

"He told me about some exercises. To make it easier for us to—" She stopped, and he waited, and she caught hold of herself and started in again. "—to consummate our marriage."

He kept his eyes on the road. He swung to the left, passed a station wagon, cut back to the right again. He looked at his hands on the steering wheel, the knuckles white, the fingers locked tight around the wheel. He moved his hands lower on the steering wheel so that she would not see them.

Suddenly he was grinning.

"Is something funny?"

"I was just picturing you," he said. "Doing your exercises."

He laughed then, and she laughed. It was the first time either of them had laughed since Carroll was murdered.

A little later he said, "There's another reason you ought to see a doctor."

"What's that?"

"I don't know how to say it. Well. Suppose you're pregnant?"

She didn't say anything.

"It's no fun to think about," he said. "But it could be. Jesus."

"Oh, Dave—"

He slowed the car. "It's nothing to worry about," he said. "They can always do something about it. The legal question varies from state to state, but I know a dozen doctors who wouldn't worry about the law. If a . . . rape victim is pregnant, she can get an abortion. There's no problem."

"Oh, God," she said. "I didn't even think. You've been worrying about this, haven't you? All night, probably."

"Well—"

"I'm not pregnant. I'm taking these pills, oral contraceptives. That was one of my surprises for you. The doctor gave me pills to take. Little yellow pills. I couldn't possibly be pregnant."

She began to cry then. He started to pull off the road but she told him to go on driving, that she would be all right. He went on driving, and she stopped crying. "Don't worry about me," she said. "I'm not going to cry any more, at all."

They made good time. They stopped once on the road for gas and food and were in New York by twelve-thirty. They came in on the Saw Mill River Parkway and the West Side Drive. They took a room with twin beds at the Royalton, on West Forty-fourth Street. The doorman parked their car for them.

Their room was on the eleventh floor. A bellhop carried their luggage, checked the towels, showed them where their closets were, opened a window, thanked Dave for the tip, and left. Dave walked to the window. You couldn't see much from it, just the side of an office building.

"We're here," he said.

"Yes. Have you spent much time in New York?"

"A couple of weekends during college. And then for six

weeks two years ago. I was studying for the bar exams, and there's a course you take just to cram for the bar. A six-week cram course. I stayed downtown at the Martinique and didn't do a thing but eat and sleep and study. I could have been in any city for all the attention I paid to it."

"I didn't know you then."

"No, not then. Do you know this city?"

She shook her head. "I have an aunt who lives here. A sister of my father's. She never married, and she has a job in the advertising department for one of the big department stores. Had, anyway. I don't know if she still does, I haven't seen her in years. Name some department stores."

"Jesus, I don't know. Saks, Brooks Brothers—"

"She wouldn't work at Brooks Brothers."

"Well, I don't know anything about department stores. Bonwit? Is there one called Bonwit?"

"It was Bergdorf Goodman. I remember now. We went to visit her, oh, two or three times. I was just a kid then. We didn't see her very often because my mother can't stand her. Do you think she might be a lesbian?"

"Your mother?"

"Oh, don't be an idiot. My aunt."

"How do I know?"

"I wonder. There was a lesbian in my dormitory in college."

"You told me."

"She wanted to make love to me. Did I tell you that, too?"

"Yes."

"Everybody said I should have reported her, but I didn't. I wonder if Aunt Beth is a lesbian."

"Call her up and ask her."

"Some other time. Dave?" Her face was serious now. "I think we ought to figure out what we're going to do first. How we're going to find them, the two men. We don't know anything about them."

"We know a few things."

"What?"

He had a notebook in his jacket pocket, a small loose-leaf notebook for appointments and memos. He sat down in an armchair and flipped the book open to a blank page. He took his pencil and wrote: "Joe Carroll."

"They killed a man named Joe Carroll," he said. "That's a start." She nodded, and he said, "If that was his name."

"Huh?"

"That was the name he gave us, and that was the name he used at the lodge. But he was running away, trying to hide. He might not have used his own name."

"What did the men call him?"

"I don't remember. I don't think they called him anything. I couldn't hear that much from where we were."

"Wouldn't the police know his real name?"

"The troopers?" He thought a minute. "He might have had some identification on him. They called him Carroll. They might have done that in front of us just keep from confusing us, but maybe not. Or maybe he wasn't carrying any identification."

"Or maybe they took his wallet with them."

"Maybe." He lit a cigarette. "But they would fingerprint him," he said. "They would do that much automatically, and they would send his prints to Washington, to the FBI. If he's ever been fingerprinted, then, his prints would be on file and they would get a positive identification of him."

"How could we find out?"

"If he's important, then it would be in the New York papers. If not, it would just be in the local papers. If Pomquit has a paper. Or one of the larger cities around there. Scranton—I don't know."

"Can you get Scranton papers in New York?"

"Yes. There's a newsstand in Times Square. I used to pick up Binghamton papers during that bar-exam stretch. The papers run late, but they would have them."

In the notebook he wrote: "Scranton paper."

He looked up. "Let's take it from the top. Carroll, whatever his name is, said he was in construction. And semiretired."

"He was probably just talking."

"Maybe. People usually stay close to the truth when they lie. Especially when they're lying just for the sake of convenience. Carroll wanted to be friendly with us, and he had to invent a story, not to keep anything from us, specifically, but because he couldn't tell the truth without drawing the wrong kind of attention to himself. He was probably a criminal. I got that picture from the way he talked with the two of them."

"So did I."

"But I think he was probably a criminal with some background in the construction business. A lot of rackets have legitimate front operations. You know the cigar store across from the Lafayette?"

"In Binghamton?"

"Yes. It's a bookie joint."

"I didn't know that."

"It's not exactly a secret. Everybody knows it, they operate pretty much in the open. Still, the place is a cigar store. They don't have a sign that says 'Bookie Joint,' and the man who runs it tells people he runs a cigar store, not a bookie joint. It's probably something like that with Carroll. He was probably in construction, or on the periphery of it, no matter what racket he may have had on the side."

He was talking as much to himself as to her now. If they were going to find Lee and the other man, they would do it by reasoning from the few facts and nuances at their disposal.

"Carroll did something wrong. That was why the two of them came after him. He double-crossed somebody."

"He said that he would make it good."

He nodded. "That's right. There was a name. Their boss, the one they work for. Carroll told them to tell the boss that he would make it good."

On the notebook page he changed the first entry to read: "Joe Carroll—Construction." Then he wrote: "Nassau County," which was where Carroll had said he was in business.

Jill said, "They mentioned the boss by name. Or Carroll did."

"I think Carroll did."

"I can remember it. Just a minute." He waited, and she closed her eyes and put her hands together, pressing the palms one against the other.

"Dublin," she said.

"No, that's not it."

"Dublin, it was Dublin. 'Tell Dublin that I'll make it good.' No, that's not right either."

"It's not what they said."

"Lublin, maybe?"

"I don't know."

"Well, say the sentence for me. I think I can tell if I hear it, if you say it for me. Like a visual memory, except different. Say the sentence the way he said it."

"With Lublin?"

"Yes."

He said, " 'Tell Lublin I'll make it good.' "

"That's it. I'm positive, Dave. Lublin."

He wrote: "Lublin—Boss."

"They worked for Lublin? Is that it?"

He shook his head. "I think he hired them. I don't think they were regular . . . well, employees of his. They were paid to kill Carroll. And when one of them wanted to kill us, so that we wouldn't be able to tell the police anything, the other said something about not killing anybody unless he was getting paid for it. As if they had been specifically hired to kill Carroll, to do that one job for a set fee."

"That was Lee who said that. I remember now."

He wrote: "Hired Professional Killers. Lee." He said, "I know one name—Lee. It could be his first name or his last name."

"Or a nickname," she said. "If his name is LeGrand, or something."

"It could be anything. That was all he was called, wasn't it? I didn't hear him called anything else. And he didn't call the other one anything."

"No, he didn't."

He lit a fresh cigarette. He looked at the notebook, at the neat entries one beneath the other: "Joe Carroll—Construction. Nassau County. Scranton paper. Lublin—Boss. Hired

Professional Killers. Lee." He went to the window and looked across at the office building. He wanted to look out at the city but the building was in the way. There were eight or nine million people in the city, and he was looking for two of those millions, and he couldn't even see the city itself. There was a building in the way.

"Dave."

He turned. She was next to him, her hair brushing his cheek. He put an arm around her and she drew close. Her head settled on his shoulder. For a moment he had thought of those two, lost in that huge crowd, and that it was hopeless and ridiculous. But now his arm was around her, and he remembered what they had done to her and what they had taken from her and from him. He closed his eyes and pictured both men dead.

# 4

HE MISSED THE out-of-town-newspaper stand on the first try.
He passed it on the wrong side of the street and walked to
Seventh Avenue and Forty-second, then got his bearings and
retraced his steps. The stand was at Forty-third Street, in
the island behind the Times Tower. He asked for a copy of
the Scranton morning paper. The newsie ducked into his
shack and came back with a folded copy of the Scranton
*Courier-Herald*. He looked at the date. It was Saturday's
paper.

"This the latest?"

"What is it, Saturday? That's the latest. No good?"

"I need today's."

The newsie said, "Can't do it. The bigger cities, Chicago or
Philly or Detroit, we get in the afternoon if it's a morning
paper or the next day if it's a night paper. The towns, we run

about two days behind. You want Monday's *Courier-Herald*, it would be Wednesday afternoon by the time I had it for you, maybe Thursday morning."

"I need this morning's paper. Even if it's late."

"You could use it Wednesday?"

"Yes," he said. "And tomorrow's, too."

"Yeah. Say, we only get two or three. You want 'em, I could set 'em aside for you. If you're sure you'll be coming back. Any paper I'm stuck with, then I'm stuck with it. But if you want 'em, I could hold 'em for you."

"How much are they?"

"Half a buck each."

"If I give you a dollar now, will you be sure to have a copy of each for me?"

"You don't have to pay me now."

"I'd just as soon," Dave said. He gave the man a dollar, then had to wait while the newsie scrawled out a receipt and made a note for himself on a scrap of paper.

Around the corner, he bought the New York afternoon papers at another newsstand. They didn't have any of the morning papers left. But the news of Carroll's murder wouldn't have gotten to New York in time for the morning papers anyway. He took the papers to a cafeteria on Forty-second Street, bought a cup of coffee, and sat down at an empty table. He checked very carefully and found no mention of the shooting in any of the papers. He left them on his table and went out of the cafeteria.

Two doors down, he stopped at an outdoor phone booth and flipped through two telephone directories, the one for Manhattan and the one for Brooklyn. There were seven Lublins listed in Manhattan and nine in Brooklyn, plus "Lublin's

Flowers" and "Lublin and Devlin—Bakers." The other local phone books were not there, just Manhattan and Brooklyn. He went to the Walgreen's on the corner of Seventh Avenue and Forty-second, and the store had the books for the Bronx and Queens and Staten Island. There were fourteen Lublins listed in the Bronx, six in Queens, and none in Staten Island. The Walgreen's did not have telephone books for northern New York, Long Island, or Westchester County. And Lublin might live in one of those places. There was no guarantee that he lived in the city itself.

In the classified directory—a separate book in New York, not just a section of yellow pages at the back—he turned to "Contractors, General." He looked first for "Lublin," because he had grown used to looking for Lublins, but there were no contractors listed under that name. He tried looking for "Carroll, Joseph." He found "Carroll, Jas" and "Carrel, J." He waited until one of the phone booths was empty, and then he dropped a dime in the slot and dialed the number for Carroll, Jas in Queens. A man answered. Dave said, "Is Mr. Carroll there?"

"Speaking."

He hung up quickly and tried another dime. He called Carrel, J., also in Queens, and the line was busy. He hung up. There was a woman waiting to use the booth. He let her wait. He called again, and this time a girl answered.

"Mr. Carrel, please," he said.

"Which Mr. Carrel?"

Which Mr. Carrel? He said, "I didn't know there were more than one. Was more than one."

"There are two Mr. Carrels," the girl said. "Whom did you wish to speak to?"

"What are their names?"

"We have a Mr. Jacob Carrel and a Mr. Leonard Carrel. Lennie . . . Mr. Leonard Carrel, I mean, is the son. He's not in, but Mr. Jacob Carrel—"

He hung up the phone. For the hell of it, he looked up "Joseph Carroll" in the Brooklyn book. There were listings for fourteen Joseph Carrolls in Brooklyn. He did not bother looking in the other books.

The only way was through Carroll, he thought. They had to learn who the man was. If they learned who Carroll was they could find the right Lublin, and once they got Lublin they could find the men he had hired to do the killing. It was impossible to find Carroll or Lublin or anyone else through the phone book. The city was too big. There were thirty-six Lublins listed in New York City and God knew how many more with no phones or unlisted numbers. And he had never heard the name Lublin before, even. A name he'd never heard, and there were too many of them in New York City for him to know where to begin.

She was waiting in the room at the Royalton. He told her where he had gone and what he had done. She didn't say anything.

He said, "Right now there's nothing to do but wait. There should be a story in one of the morning papers, and then there should be a longer story in the Scranton papers when we get them. Maybe we should have stayed around the lodge for a day or two, maybe we would have found out something."

"I couldn't stay there."

"No, neither could I."

"We could go to Scranton, if you want. And save a day."

He shook his head. "That's going around Robin Hood's barn. We wait. We're here, and we'll stay here. Once we find out who Carroll is, or was, then we can think of what to do."

"You think he was a gangster?"

"Something like that."

"I liked him," she said.

Around six-thirty they went across the street and had dinner at a Chinese restaurant. The food was fair. They went back to the hotel and sat in the room but it was too small, they felt too confined. There was a television set in the room. She turned it on and started watching a panel show. He got up, went over to the set, and turned it off. "Come on," he said. "Let's get out of here, let's go to a movie."

"What's playing?"

"What's the difference?"

They went to the Criterion on Broadway and saw a sexy comedy with Dean Martin and Shirley MacLaine. He bought loge tickets and they shared cigarettes and watched the movie. They got there about ten minutes after the picture started, left about fifteen minutes before it ended. On the way back to the hotel they stopped at a newsstand, and he tried to buy the morning papers. The early edition of the *Daily News* was the only one available. He bought the *News* and they went back to their room.

He divided the paper in half and they went through it. There was nothing about the murder in either section. He picked up both halves and threw them out. She asked what time it was.

"Nine-thirty."

"This takes forever," she said. "Do you want to try getting the *Times* again?"

"Not yet."

She got up and walked to the window, turned, walked to the bed, turned again and faced him. "I think I'm going crazy," she said.

He got up, walked to her. She turned from him. She said, "Like a lion in a cage."

"Easy, baby."

"Let's get drunk, Dave. Can we do that?"

Her face was calm, unreally so. Her hands, at her sides, were knotted into tight little fists with her long fingernails digging into her palms. She saw him looking at her fists, and she opened her hands. There were red marks on the palms of her hands—she had very nearly broken the skin.

He picked up the phone and got the bell captain. He ordered a bottle of V.O., ice, club soda, and two glasses. When the kid brought their order he met him at the door, took the tray from him, signed the tab, and gave the kid a dollar.

"My husband is a big tipper," she said. "How much money do we have left?"

"A couple of hundred. Enough."

He started making the drinks. She said, "How much is the hotel room?"

"I don't know. Why?"

"We could go to a cheaper hotel. We'll be here a while and we don't want to run out of money."

"They'll take a check."

"They will?"

"Any hotel will," he said. "Any halfway decent hotel."

48

She took her drink and held it awkwardly while he finished making one for himself. He raised his glass toward her and she lowered her eyes and drank part of her drink. When their glasses were empty he took them over to the dresser and added more whiskey and a little more soda.

"I'm going to get drunk tonight," she said. "I've never been really stoned in front of you, have I?"

"The hell you haven't."

"I don't mean parties. Everybody gets drunk at parties. I mean plain drinking where you're just trying to get stoned, like now. We used to at college. My roommate and I, my junior year. My roommate was a girl from Virginia named Mary Beth George. You never met her."

"No."

"We would get stoned together and tell each other all our little problems. She used to cry when she got drunk. I didn't. We swore that we would be each other's maid of honor. Or matron, whoever got married first. I didn't even invite her to the wedding. I never even thought to. Isn't that terrible?"

"Is she married?"

"I think so."

"Did she invite you to her wedding?"

"No. We lost track of each other. Isn't that the worst thing you ever heard of? We drank vodka and water. Did you ever have that?"

"Yes."

"It didn't have any taste at all. It tasted like water with too much chlorine in it, the way it gets in the winter sometimes. You know how I mean, don't you?"

"Yes."

"With a little provocation I think I could maybe become

an alcoholic. Will you make me another of these, please?"

He fixed her another drink. He made it strong, and he added a little of the V.O. to his own glass. She took several small quick sips from her drink.

She said, "I didn't even know you then. Both in Binghamton and we never even met. We went to two different schools together. That's a stupid line, isn't it? There was a comedian who used to say that, but I can't remember who. Can you?"

"No."

"There are some other lines like that. 'Would you rather go to New York or by train?' Silly. 'Do you walk to school or take your lunch?' I think that's my favorite. I didn't fall in love with you the first time I saw you. I didn't even like you. What dreadful things I'm telling you! But when you asked me out I felt very excited. I didn't know why. I thought here I don't like him, but I'm excited he asked me out. I can't stop talking. I'm just babbling like an idiot, I can't stop talking."

She drank almost all of her drink in one swallow and took a step toward him, just one step, and then stopped. There was a moment when he thought she was going to fall down and he started for her to catch her but she stayed on her feet. She had a worried look on her face.

She said, "I might be sick."

"Don't worry about it."

"I want you to make love to me, you know that, don't you? You know I want that, don't you?"

He held her and her face was pressed against his chest. She put her hands on his upper arms and pushed him away a little and looked up into his eyes. Her own eyes were a deeper green than ever, the color of fine jade.

She said, "I want to but I can't. I love you, I love you more

50

than I ever did, but I just can't do anything. Do you understand?"

"Yes. Don't talk about it."

"This afternoon I thought I would wait for you and when you came back I would get you to make love to me, and everything would be all right. You haven't tried to make love to me. I think if you'd tried, before, I would have gone crazy. I don't know. But I sat here in this room and I planned it out, all of it, and just what I would do and just how I would feel, and I was all alone in the room, and all of a sudden I started to shake. I couldn't do it. Oh, I'm afraid."

"Don't be."

"Will I be all right?"

"Yes."

"How can you tell?"

"I know."

"I think you're right. I think everything's just stopped, just shut up in a box, until we do what we have to do. Those men. I can shut my eyes and see their faces perfectly. If I knew how to draw I could draw them, every detail. I'll be all right afterward, I think."

A few minutes later she said, "This is some honeymoon, isn't it? I'm sorry, darling." Then he took her into the bathroom and held her while she threw up. She was very sick and he held her and told her it was all right, everything was all right. He helped her wash up and he undressed her and put her to bed. She did not cry at all through any of this. He put her to bed and covered her with the sheet and the blanket and she looked up at him and said that she loved him, and he kissed her. She was asleep almost at once.

He had one more drink, no soda and no ice. He capped the

bottle and put it in the dresser with his shirts. In the morning, he thought, he would have to take a bundle to the laundry, the two shirts he had worn and a pair of slacks. And he would have to buy some things if he got the chance. He had packed mostly sportswear for the stay at the lodge and he would need dress shirts in New York.

The liquor helped him sleep. He woke up very suddenly and looked at his watch and it was seven o'clock, he had slept eight hours. He got dressed and went downstairs and outside. Jill was still sleeping. He bought the morning newspapers and went back to the room, and one of them had the story.

# 5

<<<<<<<<<<<<<<<<<<<<<<<<<<<<<<<<<<<<<<<<<<<<<<<<<<<

### Pennsylvania Shooting Victim
### Identified As Hicksville Builder

Scranton, Pa.—State police today identified the
victim of a vicious gangland-style slaying as
Joseph P. Corelli, a Long Island building con-
tractor residing in Hicksville.

Corelli was shot to death late Sunday in an
as yet unsolved attack outside his cabin at Pomquit Lodge on nearby Lake Wallenpaupack. "It
has all the earmarks of a professional murder,"
stated Sheriff Roy Fairland of Pomquit. "Corelli
was shot five times in the head and two different
guns were used."

The dead man had resided at Pomquit Lodge
for almost three months prior to the murder. He
was registered at the Lodge as Joseph Carroll
and carried false identification in that name.
Proper identification of Corelli was facilitated

through fingerprint records of the Federal Bureau of Investigation.

Corelli was arrested three times in the past five years, twice on charges of extortion and once for possession of betting slips. He was released each time without being brought to trial, according to New York Police Sgt. James Gregg. "He [Corelli] had definite underworld connections," Sgt. Gregg asserted. "He had several criminal contacts that we know of, and it's a good bet he was operating outside the law."

Nassau County police officials denied knowledge of any recent criminal activity on Corelli's part. "We were aware of his record and kept an eye on him," one officer stated, "but if he was involved in anything shady, it was going on outside of our jurisdiction."

Corelli, a bachelor, lived alone at 4113 Bayview Road in Hicksville and maintained an office in the Bascom Building, also in Hicksville. His sole survivor is a sister, Mrs. Raymond Romagno of Boston.

When he opened the door of the hotel room she sat up in the bed and blinked at him. Her face was pale and drawn. He asked her if she was all right.

"I'm a little rocky," she said. "I drank too much, I got all sloppy. I'm sorry."

"Forget it. It's in the paper."

"Carroll?"

"Corelli," he said. He folded the paper open to the story and handed it to her. She couldn't find it at first and he sat next to her and pointed it out to her. He watched her face while she worked her way through the article. Halfway through she motioned for a cigarette and he lit one for her. She coughed on it but went on reading to the end of the article. Then she set the paper on the bed beside her. She finished the cigarette and put it out in the ashtray on top of the bedside table. She started to say something, then realized for the first time that she didn't have any clothes on. She looked at herself and jumped up and ran into the bathroom.

When she came out she looked reborn. Her face was fresh and clean, the pallor gone from it now. She had lipstick on. He smoked a cigarette while she put on a dress and shoes.

She said, "Corelli. I didn't think he looked Italian."

"He could have been almost anything, as far as I could tell. He didn't look Irish, either."

"Carroll isn't always Irish."

"I guess not."

"There was a composer named Corelli. Before Bach, I think. We were right about almost everything, weren't we? About who he was. He was in construction, but he was also a gangster."

"In a small way." He thought a minute. "There are some things that aren't in that article.

"You mean about us?"

"I mean about Carroll. Corelli. What rackets he was in, who his friends were. They talked a lot about his contacts but they didn't say who they were. It might help to know."

"How do we find out?"

"From the police," he said.

"You mean just ask them?"

"Not exactly," he said.


They skipped breakfast. They left the hotel and found an empty phone booth in a drugstore on Sixth Avenue. He coached her on what to say and she practiced while he looked up the number of police headquarters in the Manhattan book. He wrote the number in his notebook and she said, "Let me try it now. How does this sound?"

He listened while she went through her speech. Then he said, "I think that's right. It's hard to tell without hearing it over the phone. Let's give it a try."

She went into the booth and closed the door. She dialed the number he had written down. A man answered in the middle of the first ring.

She said, "Sergeant James Gregg, please. Long distance calling."

The man asked her who was calling. She said, "The Scranton *Courier-Herald*."

The man told her to hang on, he'd see if he could find Gregg. There was a pause, and some voices in the distance, and a click and silence, another click and a youngish voice saying, "Gregg here."

"Sergeant James Gregg?"

"Speaking."

"Go ahead, please." She opened the phone-booth door quickly, stepped outside and handed the receiver to Dave. He took it, ducked into the booth and pulled the door shut.

He said, "Sergeant Gregg? This is Pete Miller at the *Courier-Herald*. We're trying to work up a background story on the Corelli murder, and I'd like to ask you a couple of questions."

"Again? I just talked to you people an hour ago."

"I just came on," he said quickly. "What we're trying to do, Sergeant Gregg, what I'm trying to do, is to work up a human-interest piece on Corelli. Gangland killings, in this area, they're exciting—"

"Exciting?"

"—and people are interested. Could you tell me a few things about Corelli?"

"Well, I'm pretty busy now."

"It won't take a minute, Sergeant. Now, first of all, I think you or somebody else mentioned that Corelli was connected with the underworld."

"He had connections," Gregg said guardedly.

"What sort of racket was he in?"

There was a short pause. Then, "What he was in was construction. We don't know exactly what he did on the side, the illegal side. He knew a lot of gamblers, and his last arrest was here in Manhattan, he was picked up in a gambling raid. We didn't have a case against him and we let him go."

"I see."

"His business was all out on Long Island. That's out of our jurisdiction, and we didn't nose around in that connection. We know he was in touch with some people here in the city, some racket people, but we don't know what exactly he was doing. If he was working a racket in Long Island, well, that wasn't our business."

"Could you tell me some of his associates in New York?"

"Why?"

"It would give the story some color," he said.

"The names wouldn't mean anything to you," Gregg said. "You're out in Scranton and Corelli's friends, the ones we know about, are just small-time gamblers. People like George White and Eddie Mizell, just people nobody ever heard of. No one important."

"I see," he said. "How about a man named Lublin?"

"Maurie Lublin? What about him?"

"Was he an associate of Corelli's?"

"Where did you hear that?"

"The name came up, I don't remember where. Was he?"

"I never heard about it. It might be. People like Corelli know a lot of people, it's hard to say. Offhand I would say Maurie Lublin is too big to be interested in Corelli."

"Do you know why Corelli was killed?"

"Well, it's not our case. There's nothing certain. Just rumors."

"Rumors?"

"That's right."

It was like pulling teeth, he thought. He said, "What kind of rumors?"

"He was supposed to owe money."

"To anyone in particular?"

"We don't know, and I wouldn't want to say anyway. Jesus, don't you people ever get together on anything? I talked to one of your men and told him most of this just a little while ago. Can't you get it from him?"

"Well, you probably talked to someone on straight news, Sergeant Gregg. I'm on features."

"Oh."

"I don't want to keep you, I know you're busy. Just one thing more. Will you be in charge of the investigation in New York?"

"Investigation?"

"Of the Corelli murder."

"What investigation?" Gregg seemed almost irritated. "He was a man from Long Island who got himself killed out of state. We're not doing anything about it. We'll cooperate

with Pennsylvania if they ask us to, but we're not doing anything."

"Will there be an investigation in Hicksville?"

"On the Island? What for? He got shot out of state, for
God's sake."

He thought, Pennsylvania would shelve it because Corelli
was from New York, and New York would forget about it
because the murder happened in Pennsylvania. He said,
"Thank you very much, Sergeant. You've been a big help,
and I didn't mean to take too much of your time."

"It's okay," Gregg said. "We try to cooperate."

He got out of the booth. She started to ask him a question,
but he shook his head and began writing in the little notebook. He wrote: "Maurie Lublin." Under that he wrote:
"George White and Eddie Mizell." On the next line he wrote:
"Corelli owed money." Then: "No Investigation."

The drugstore was too crowded to talk in. He took her
arm, put the notebook back in his breast pocket, and led her
out of the store. There was a Cobb's Corner across the
street. They waited for the light to change, crossed Sixth
Avenue and went into the restaurant. It was past nine already. Most of the breakfast crowd had gone to work and the
place was near empty. They took a table for two in the rear
and ordered orange juice and toast and coffee. He gave her
the whole conversation by the time the waitress brought the
food.

"You'd make a good reporter," she said.

"And you'd make a good telephone operator. I kept waiting for him to catch on and start wondering who the hell I
was and why I was bothering him, but he believed it all
the way. We learned a lot."

"Yes."

"A hell of a lot. George White and Eddie Mizell—I don't know what we can do with those names. But there is a Lublin. And he's a crook, and he's in New York somewhere. Maurie Lublin. Maurice, I guess that would be."

"Or Morris."

"One or the other. And everything still holds together the way we figured it. That Joe Corelli owed money, I mean. And that was why he was running."

She nodded and sipped her coffee. He lit a cigarette and set it down in an oval glass ashtray.

"The big thing is that there's no investigation. Not in New York and not in Hicksville. Isn't that a hell of a name for a town?"

"Probably a description."

"Probably. But the cops there won't bother with the murder. They may close a file on Corelli but that's all. That means we go out there."

"To Hicksville?"

"That's right."

"Is that safe?"

"It's safe. There won't be any police there, not at his place and not at his office either. The New York police aren't interested in Corelli any more. And Lublin's men won't be there, either."

"How do you know?"

"They had about three months to search Corelli's room and office. Maybe that was how they found out where he was, how they got the idea. That lodge was out of the way. They must have had some information or they never would have dug him up. They've probably sifted through his papers and everything else a dozen times already. Now he's out of the way. They won't be interested any more."

She looked thoughtful. He said, "Maybe you should stay at the hotel, baby. I'll run out there myself."

"No."

"It won't take long. And—"

"No. Whither thou goest and all that. That's not it. I was just wondering what we could find there. If they already searched—"

"They were looking for different things. They wanted to find out where Corelli was hiding, and we want to find out why he was hiding, and from whom. It's worth a try."

"And I'm going with you, Dave."

He argued some more and got nowhere with it. He let it go. It seemed safe enough, and perhaps she'd be better off with him than alone with her thoughts at the hotel.

The doorman at the Royalton got the car for them. He told them how to find the Queens-Midtown tunnel and what to do when they were through it. The sky was clouded over and the air was thick with the promise of rain. They drove through the tunnel and cut east across Queens on an expressway. The road was confusing. They missed the turnoff for Hicksville, went five miles out of their way and cut back. At an Atlantic station they filled the gas tank and found out where Bayview Road was. They hit Bayview Road in the 2300 block and drove past numbered streets until they found the address listed in the newspaper story. Hicksville was monolithic, block after block of semidetached two-story brick houses with treeless front yards and a transient air, a general impression that all the inhabitants were merely living there until they could afford to move again, either further out on the Island or closer to the city.

Corelli's building, 4113, was another faceless brick building jammed between 4111 and 4115. There were wash lines in the back. According to the mailboxes, someone named Haas lived upstairs and someone named Penner lived on the ground floor. Dave stepped back into the street to check the address, then dug the newspaper clipping from his wallet to make sure he had read it correctly the first time around: "Corelli, a bachelor, lived alone at 4113 Bayview Road in Hicksville . . ."

Jill told him to try the downstairs buzzer. "Probably the landlord," she said. "They buy the house and live downstairs and rent out the upstairs. The income covers the mortgage payments."

He rang the downstairs bell and waited. There were sounds inside the house but nothing happened. He rang again, and a muffled voice called, "All right, I'm coming, take it easy."

He waited. The door opened inward and a woman peered suspiciously at him through the screen door. Her face said she thought he was a salesman and she wasn't interested. Then she caught sight of Jill and decided that he wasn't a salesman and her face softened slightly. She still wasn't thrilled to see him, her face said, but at least he wasn't selling anything, and that was a break.

He said, "Mrs. Penner?"

She nodded. He searched for the right phrasing, something that would fit whether or not she knew Corelli was dead. "My name is Peter Miller," he said. "Does a Mr. Joseph Corelli live in the upstairs apartment?"

"Why?"

"Just business," he said, smiling.

"He used to live here. I rented the place after he skipped on me. He lives here for three years, he pays his rent every time the first of the month, and then he skips. Just one day he's gone." She shook her head. "Just disappears. Didn't take his things, that's his furniture and he left it, everything. I figured he would be back. Leaving everything, you would think he'd be back, wouldn't you?"

He nodded. She didn't know Corelli was dead, he thought. Maybe that was good.

"But he never shows," she said, shifting conveniently into present tense again. "He never shows, and I hold the place a month, waiting for him. That's seventy dollars I'm out plus another week before I could rent it. I don't rent to colored and it took a full week before they moved in, Mr. and Mrs. Haas. Eighty-five dollars he cost me, Corelli."

"Do you have his things? His furniture and all?"

"I rented the place furnished," Mrs. Penner said. She was defensive now. "Mrs. Haas, she didn't have any furniture. They just got married. No kids, you know?" She shook her head again. "There'll be kids, though. A young couple, they'll have kids soon enough, you bet on it. One thing about Corelli, he was quiet up there. What about his things? He send you or something?"

Jill said, "Mrs. Penner, I'm Joe's sister. Joe called me, he's in Arizona and he had to leave New York in a hurry."

"Cop trouble?"

"He didn't say. Mrs. Penner—"

"There was cops came around right after he left. Showed me their badges and went pawing through everything." She paused. "They don't look like cops, not them. But they show

63

me their badges and that's enough. I don't like to stick my nose in."

Jill said, "Mrs. Penner, you know Joe was in business here. There was a lawsuit and he had to leave the state to stay out of trouble. It wasn't police trouble."

"So?"

"He called me yesterday," she went on. "There were some things of his, some things he had to leave here, and he wanted me to get them for him."

"Sure."

"If I could just—"

The screen door stayed shut. "As soon as I get that eighty-five dollars," she said. "That's what he cost me, that eighty-five dollars. There was no lease so that's all, just the eighty-five, but I want that before he gets his stuff."

Jill didn't say anything. Dave took out a cigarette and said, "You can hold the furniture for the time being, Mrs. Penner. In fact I think Joe would just as soon you kept the furniture, and then you can go on renting the flat furnished. It's worth more than eighty-five dollars, but just to make things easier you could keep the furniture for the rent you missed out on."

He could see her mind working, balancing the extra five or ten dollars a month against the eighty-five dollars Corelli had cost her. She looked as though she wanted a little more, so he said, "Unless you'd rather have the money. Then I could have a truck here later this afternoon to pick up the furniture."

He could imagine her trying to explain that to the Haases. Quickly she said, "No, it's fair enough. And easier all around, right?"

"That's what I thought. Now if we could see Joe's other stuff, his clothes and all. You kept everything, didn't you?"

She had everything downstairs in large cardboard boxes. Suits, ties, slacks, underwear. Corelli had had an extensive wardrobe, sharp Broadway suits with Phil Kronfeld and Martin Janss labels in them. There was one boxful of papers. Dave took the carton and carried it out to the car. Jill waited in the car, and he went back to the house and told Mrs. Penner he would send somebody around for the rest of the stuff, the clothes and everything. "Today or tomorrow," he said.

That was fine with her. He got into the car and drove off.

At the Bascom Building, in Hicksville's business district, Jill waited in the car with the box of papers while he went inside and managed to get into Corelli's office. This was easier, because they hadn't moved him out for nonpayment of rent. He had been gone for three months but they had left his office as he had left it, the door locked and everything undisturbed. He found the superintendent and told him he wanted to get into Corelli's office, and the old man said he had to have the key or written authorization.

Dave gave him a story off the top of his head—that Corelli had sent him down to pick up copies of a contract, that it would only be for a minute, and that he didn't want to take the time to get a written authorization from Corelli. The super didn't believe it but he just nodded, waiting. Dave gave him ten dollars and the super made the bill disappear and took him upstairs and unlocked the door for him. He seemed to be doing something he had done before—for the men who had been looking for Corelli.

65

"Don't be long now," he said. "And lock the door behind you, hear?"

He wasn't long. The office was a cubbyhole, one window facing out on the main street of Hicksville, a single dark-green filing cabinet, a cheap oak desk, a standing coatrack. The wooden desk chair was padded with a cushion that smelled slightly of old rubber.

There were three drawers to the filing cabinet. The bottom drawer held a half-full bottle of Philadelphia blended whiskey. The middle drawer was empty. In the top drawer there was a disorganized pile of contracts and invoices and letters. The letterheads, as far as he could see, were of various companies in the building trades. He shuffled all the papers into a moderately neat pile and stuffed them into a brown manila envelope.

The desktop was free from clutter. There was a thick layer of dust across it but nothing else. In the top drawer of the desk he found a box of paper clips, a year-old copy of *Argosy* folded open to an article on skin-diving paraphernalia, a memo pad with no entries in it, a Zippo cigarette lighter initialed "J.C.," a four- by five-inch glossy print of a girl in panties and bra, a pigskin address book, and a packet of contraceptives. He added the address book to the manila envelope and closed the drawer. In another drawer, far in the rear, he found an unloaded gun and, behind it, a nearly full box of cartridges.

He picked up the gun, then stopped and glanced automatically at the window. No one was watching him, of course. He hefted the gun and felt its weight. He hesitated just a moment, then tucked the gun into his pants pocket. the right-hand pocket. He put the box of shells in his left-hand jacket pocket, stopped, lit a cigarette, and checked the one remaining drawer in the desk. It was empty, and he closed it and straightened up.

Outside, it was getting ready to rain. He got behind the wheel and Jill asked him if there had been anything important in the office. He told her he didn't know yet, that they would have to see. She said she had forgotten how to get back to the city and asked him if he remembered the route. He started the car and told her that he remembered the way.

# 6

<<<<<<<<<<<<<<<<<<<<<<<<<<<<<<<<<<<<<<<<<<<<<<<<<<<

THE GUN WAS a Bodyguard, by Smith & Wesson. It was a five-shot revolver that took .38-Special shells, and it was hammerless, so you didn't have to cock it—a pull on the trigger would fire the gun. It had a two-inch barrel, it was black, it was steel, it weighed a pound and a quarter. The grip was textured, and formed to fit the hand.

The purpose of the gun was implicit in its design. Because it was short-barreled, its accuracy was somewhat limited; it would be a poor bet for target shooting or long-range plinking. The short barrel meant that it was designed to be carried easily on the person, probably concealed. The absence of a hammer facilitated quick draws; a hammer might catch on clothing, might leave the gun snagged in a pocket or under a belt. The gun had been made to carry, to fire easily and quickly, to shoot ammunition that would kill a man with a well-placed hit. It was a gun for killing people.

Now, it was unloaded. He sat on the edge of the bed in their hotel room and held the gun in his right hand, his hand curled around the butt, his finger just resting lightly upon the trigger. The box of shells was on the bed beside him. He opened the box and loaded the gun, putting shells in four of the five chambers. He rotated the cylinder so that there was no cartridge under the hammer and so that nothing would happen if the trigger was pulled accidentally.

He looked up. Jill's eyes were on the gun, and they were nervous. She raised her eyes to meet his.

"Dave, do you know how to use that?"

"Yes." He looked at the gun again, set it down on the bed beside him. He closed the box of ammunition. "In the army. They taught us guns. In basic training. Mostly rifles, of course, but there was a brief course on handguns."

She didn't say anything. He picked up a stack of papers and ruffled through them. They had gone through everything in less than an hour, finding almost all of Corelli's papers less than useless. The business papers might have been clues to something, but they couldn't tell—they were just various bills and receipts and letters relating to Corelli's construction business. He had evidently been something of a middleman in construction, setting up jobs and parceling them out among subcontractors.

The personal papers included a slew of IOU's, around a dozen of them representing money owed to Corelli, debts canceled now by his death. They ranged from thirty-five dollars to one for an even thousand, with most of them running around a hundred. There were four rather stiff letters from the sister in Boston, written neatly in dark-blue ink, telling him about her husband and her children and her house and asking him how business was going. There were irritatingly obscure little bits of memoranda—telephone numbers, addresses, names, none linked to anything in particular, each of them standing alone on its own sheet of paper: "Room 417 Barbizon Plaza"; "Henrich, 45 @ 7½ = $337.50"; "Flowers for Joanie"—a few tickets on losing horses that had run at Aqueduct, at Belmont, at Roosevelt.

In the address book, there were more than fifty entries, most of them tersely inscribed with initials or just a first name or just a last name. There were seventeen girls listed only by first name and telephone number, no address, no last name. Maurie Lublin was listed by last name alone, with a phone number and no address.

Several slips of paper contained just numbers—columns of figures, isolated numbers, bits of addition and subtraction. The number 65,000 came up on several sheets, twice with a dollar sign: $65,000.

Dave said, "Sixty-five thousand dollars. That must be what he owed."

"To Lublin?"

"I suppose so. I don't know whether he stole it or owed it. Lee and the other one didn't find that money, so he didn't take it with him. If he had it, and he was running away, wouldn't he have taken the money with him? I think he must have owed it to Lublin and then couldn't pay. He left town in a hurry, not as though he had planned it or anything. I think he owed the money and planned on paying it, and then he couldn't pay it and he panicked and ran. And they found him."

"And killed him."

"Yes."

She sat next to him on the bed. The gun was between them, and she looked down at it and said, "Guns scare me."

"Pick it up."

"Why?"

"Pick it up." She did. He showed her how to hold it and made her curl her index finger around the trigger. "Aim at the doorknob," he said.

She aimed. He sighted along the barrel and showed her how her aim was off, and taught her how to line up a target. He took the gun from her and spilled out the shells, clearing all five chambers. Then he made her aim at the doorknob and squeeze the trigger to get the feel of the gun. After she practiced for a few minutes he took the gun from her and loaded it again.

He said, "There's only one way. We could try to dig up Corelli's life history if we wanted. We could call up each of the girls he knew and find out what they all knew about him. We could look him up in the *New York Times* file, and we could look up all the people in his address book, and we could find out everything there is to know about Joe Corelli."

"Is that what you want to do?"

"No." He took out two cigarettes, lit one for himself and offered the other to her. She shook her head and he put the cigarette back in the pack. "No," he said again. "Corelli doesn't matter any more. We're not trying to find Corelli. He's dead, and we don't need him. We're not writing his biography. We're looking for the two other men."

She didn't say anything.

"Lublin hired those men," he said. "We have Lublin's name and we have his phone number. We can find out where he lives. We'll see him, and he'll tell us who the men were who killed Corelli."

"Why will he tell us?"

"We'll make him tell us."

Her eyes darted to the gun, then away. She said, "Now?"

"Now." He stood up, gun in hand. "We'll check the drugstore phone books. We'll find the Lublin who matches the number in Corelli's book, and then we'll go see him."

Dave tried the gun in each of his jacket pockets. In the inside pockets, it made a revealing bulge. In the outside pockets it hung loose and awkward. He jammed it under his belt but it didn't feel right there, either.

Jill said, "Give it to me." He gave her the gun and she put it in her purse. The purse was a flat one, black calf, and the gun did not fit well. She got another purse from the dresser, a larger one, and she put the gun and her other things into it. There was no bulge this time.

It was raining now, raining steadily, with a wind whipping the rain into their faces as they walked to the drugstore. Cars streaked by on wet asphalt. She held his arm with one hand and the purse with the other. In the drugstore, he started to look through all the phone books. She saved time by calling Information and asking the operator which borough Lublin's exchange would be in. The exchange was Ulster 9, and the operator told her that would be in Brooklyn.

They found him in the Brooklyn phone book: "Lublin, Maurice 4412 Nwkrk . . . ULster 9-2459." He looked at the listing and couldn't figure out what the street was supposed

to be. There was a New York street directory on the magazine rack, and he thumbed back to the index and checked
the Brooklyn streets in alphabetical order. There was a Newkirk Avenue listed; it was the only street that fit.

He tried Lublin's number, and no one answered. He called
again and got no answer, then checked the phone book
again to see if there was an office listed. There wasn't.

"He's not home," he told her.

"Then let's have dinner. I'm starving."

He was, too. They hadn't eaten at all since morning, and
it was almost six already. But he hadn't noticed his hunger
until she mentioned it. He interpreted this as a sign of their
progress. They were moving now, growing involved in the
mechanics of pursuit, and he had been hungry without even
realizing it.

They went to an Italian restaurant down the block and
ate lasagne and drank bottles of beer. In the middle of the
meal he left the table and used the phone to dial Lublin's
number. There was no answer. He came back to the table
and told her.

"He'll get home eventually," she said.

"I suppose so."

After dinner, he called again. There was no answer. They
stopped at a drugstore and bought a couple of magazines,
and he tried again on the drugstore phone. No answer. They
went back to the hotel room. At seven-thirty he tossed a magazine aside and picked up the phone, then cradled it.

"What's the matter?"

"I don't know," he said. "Do you suppose they listen in?"

"Who?"

"The hotel operators."

"Maybe."

"I'll be back in a minute."

He went downstairs and around the corner to the drug-store and tried again. There was no answer. In the hotel room, he kept looking at his watch. He went back to the drug-store again at eight, and called, and a man answered.

He said, "Mr. Lublin?"

"Just a minute, I'll get him." Then, "Maurie. For you."

He hung up and went back to the room. He told her, "Lub-lin's home now but he's not alone. Somebody else answered the phone."

"Was it—"

"No, I'm sure it wasn't. I'd remember their voices." He thought a moment. "There were noises in the background. They may have been having a party. I don't know. I think there were a lot of people there. But there's at least one other man, the one who answered the phone. And he called Lublin by name. If Lublin were the only other person there, he wouldn't have called him by name, I don't think."

"What do we do now?"

"I'll call again in a little while. Sooner or later he'll be the only one left, and then I'll go after him."

She didn't say anything for several minutes. Then she said, "Don't call again tonight."

"Why not?"

"Because he'll be suspicious. Calling and then hanging up —if it just happens once he'll shrug it off, but if it happens more than that he'll get suspicious. We can't let him be on guard. The best thing for us right now is that nobody even

75

knows about us. Lublin doesn't know we exist and the two men don't know we're looking for them. We can't afford to let them find out."

She was right. "I'll go there around three in the morning," he said. "The party'll be over by then."

"No."

"Why not, Jill?"

"He might not live alone." She sat next to him and held his hands in hers. "Please," she said. "We don't know anything about him yet, about the setup there. Let's wait until tomorrow. We can go there after a call, or if nobody's home we can go there and break in and wait for him. Either way. Right now he's there and he has company, and we don't even know if he lives in a house or an apartment, we don't know anything. Can't we wait until morning?"

"Are you nervous?"

"Partly. And I'm exhausted, for another thing. A good sleep wouldn't hurt either of us. Tomorrow—"

He nodded slowly. She was right, there was no sense wasting their major advantage of surprise. And it wouldn't hurt to wait another day. They had plenty of time.

He got the bottle of V.O. from the drawer and lay on the bed with it. She went over and turned on the television set. There was a doctor program on, something about an immigrant who wouldn't consent to surgery, and they watched it together. He didn't pay very much attention to it. He stretched out on the bed and sipped the V.O. straight from the bottle, not working hard at it but just sipping as he watched the program. She said she didn't want anything to drink.

After that, they watched a cops-and-robbers thing for an hour, then caught the eleven o'clock news. There was nothing important on the news. During the weather report she turned off the television set and suggested that they go to sleep. He was tired without being sleepy. He could feel the exhaustion in his body, the need for sleep, but at the same time he felt entirely awake. But sleep was a good idea. He took another long swig from the bottle to make sleep come easier.

They undressed in the same room with no embarrassment, no need for privacy. The adjustment of the honeymoon, he thought wryly. They had accomplished that much, surely. There was no longer any question of embarrassment. He felt that he could not possibly be embarrassed now in front of this woman, that they had lived through too much together, had shared too much, had grown too intimate to be separated by that variety of distance. They undressed, and he switched on the bedside lamp and turned off the overhead light, and they got into bed, and he switched off the bedside lamp and they lay together in darkness.

She was breathing very heavily. He moved toward her and she flowed into his arms and her mouth was warm and eager. He kissed her and felt her warmth against him, and he kissed her again and touched her sleeping breasts and she said his name in a husky whisper. His hands were filled with the sweet flesh.

It didn't work. It began well, but there was tension for him and tension for her and it did not work at all. The desire was there but the capacity was not.

She lay very close to him. "I'm sorry," she said.

77

"Shhhh."

"I love you. We were married Sunday. What's today? Tuesday night? We've only been married two days."

He didn't say anything.

"Two days," she said. "It seems so long. I don't think I knew you at all when we got married. Not at all. Courtship, engagement, all of that, and I hardly knew you. And two days."

He kissed her lightly.

"I love you," she said. "Sleep."

He lay in the darkness, sure he wouldn't sleep. Lublin was in Brooklyn, on Newkirk Avenue. He had called him on the phone, had hung up before Lublin could take the call. He should have waited another minute, he thought. Just long enough to hear the man's voice so he would know it.

But it was real now, it was all real. Before there had been the fury, the need to Do Something, but the reality had not been present. And then that day there had been the article in the paper, the visual proof again of Corelli's death. And the trip to Hicksville, to Corelli's home and to Corelli's office.

It was very real. He had a gun now, Corelli's gun, and all he knew about a gun was what he had learned ages ago in basic training. Could he hit anything with a gun? Could he use it properly?

And he had never fired at a human target. Not with a revolver, not with a rifle, not with anything. He had never aimed at a living person and tried to kill that person.

He reached out a hand and lightly touched his wife's body. She did not stir. He drew his hand back, then, and settled himself in the bed and took a deep breath.

He woke up very suddenly. He had fallen asleep without expecting to, and now he woke up as though he had been dynamited from the bed. His mouth was dry and his head ached dully. He sat bolt upright in the bed and tried to catch his breath. He was out of breath, as if he had been running furiously for a bus.

His cigarettes were on the bedside table. He reached out and got the pack, shook out a cigarette, lit it, cupping the flame to avoid awakening Jill. The smoke was strong in his lungs. He smothered a cough, breathed in air, then drew once more on the cigarette.

He looked at her side of the bed and could not see her in the darkness. He reached out a tentative hand to touch her.

She was not there.

In the bathroom, then. He called her name, and there was no answer, no answer.

"Jill!"

Nothing. He got out of bed and went to the bathroom. It was empty. He turned on lights, looked around for a note. No note.

She was gone.

# 7

The desk clerk said, "Mrs. Wade left about a half hour ago, sir. Or maybe a little more than that. Let me see, I came on at midnight, and then I had a cup of coffee at two-thirty, and then your wife left the hotel just as I was finishing my coffee. It must have been a quarter to three, I would guess." It was just three-thirty now. Forty-five minutes, he thought. Jill had been gone for forty-five minutes.

"Is anything wrong, Mr. Wade?"

"No," he said. "Nothing's wrong." He forced a smile. "She probably couldn't sleep," he said. "Probably went out for coffee."

He went back upstairs and sat in the room and smoked another cigarette. Jill was gone. Jill had gotten up in the middle of the night, alone, and had dressed and left. For coffee?

It was possible, he guessed. But for three-quarters of an hour?

She had left the hotel by herself. The immediate fear, the automatic reaction once he realized she was gone, was the worry that someone had come to take her away. But that was senseless. No one knew about either of them, no one knew where they were staying. And no one had called their room, either. He would have heard the phone no matter how deeply he was sleeping, for one thing. And the desk clerk would probably have mentioned a call.

He checked the whiskey bottle. It was as full as it had been. If she wanted a drink, he thought, she would have had it there. She wouldn't go barhopping by herself in the middle of the night. Coffee, then. Coffee and a sandwich, maybe.

Why hadn't she come back?

He put on a coat and went down to the lobby and out into the night. It was still raining, but the rain had slowed to a drizzle. Most of the lights were out on Forty-fifth Street. He walked to the corner of Sixth. The Cobb's Corner was open, and he went inside and looked around, but she wasn't there. He went out again and stood on the corner in the rain, looking around, trying to figure out where she might be. There were three or four open restaurants that he could see and, along Sixth Avenue, more than a dozen bars. She could be anywhere. Or she could be somewhere else, and not in any of these places.

Check them all? It didn't make any sense. And suppose she wanted to get in touch with him, and called him, and he wasn't there. Or suppose she got back to the hotel while he was out looking for her.

He went back to the Royalton. He sat in a chair, and then he got up suddenly and looked for her purse. The large brown purse was on a chair. He opened it, and saw the gun; she had left it behind. But the purse was empty otherwise, and he guessed that she had transferred everything to the black-calf purse before leaving.

Where could she have gone? Just out for coffee, he told himself. Just out for coffee, and if he would just sit back and relax she would return to the room in no time at all. But he couldn't make himself believe it. She wouldn't be gone this long.

He remembered again, unwillingly now, the sudden rush of reality that had come that night after the call to Lublin. The quick and certain proof that this was no game they were playing, no treasure hunt. That, and then the unsuccessful attempt to make love.

And he thought, We never should have come. We should have left that place and gone somewhere else until the honeymoon was over, and then we should have gone back to Binghamton. No pursuit, no chase, no revenge. We should have gone home.

Because he knew, now, what had happened. Jill had panicked. The initial shock of violation had steeled her, had made her determination for revenge equal to his own, but by now her reactions had cooled and jelled and had changed from determination to panic. He remembered the look in her eyes when he had taught her to use the gun, and he remembered the way she had wanted to wait a day before going after Lublin. Panic, panic. The hunt was wrong for a woman, for a girl; she was no huntress, no killer, and she had not been able to take it, and now she was gone.

Where? Back to Binghamton, he thought. Back to her home, where she knew everyone and where she would be safe. He had misjudged her and now she was running, and he paced the floor of their room and tried to figure out what to do next. At one point he started to pack their clothes into their suitcases, then suddenly changed his mind and put everything back where it had been. He took the gun from her purse and held it first in one hand and then in the other, switching it nervously back and forth, finally sighing and returning it to the large brown bag.

Twice he picked up the bottle of V.O. and each time he put it back without drinking. One time he uncapped it. The other time he just held it in both hands and looked at the amber whiskey.

At twenty minutes after four, the phone rang. He was sitting right next to it, sitting on the edge of the bed. When it rang he dropped a cigarette onto the rug. He didn't bother to pick it up but ground it into the carpet while he reached for the phone.

"Dave? Did I wake you?"

"My God, where are you?"

"I'm calling from a drugstore. Relax, darling. I'm all right. I didn't mean to frighten you, but—"

"Where are you?"

"Get a pencil."

He started to say something, changed his mind and got up. His pen and his little notebook were on the top of the dresser. He got them and opened the notebook and said, "All right. Where are you?"

"A drugstore. It's on the corner of Flatbush Avenue and Ditmas Avenue—that's in Brooklyn."

"What are you—"

She cut in on him. "Get in a cab," she said easily. "Come

here as soon as you can. I'll be waiting right here, in the store. And bring the thing in my brown purse. All right?"

"Jill—"

"Flatbush and Ditmas," she said. "I'm sorry if I worried you, darling. And hurry."

# 8

>>>>>>>>>>>>>>>>>>>>>>>>>>>>>>>>>>>>>>>>>>>>>>

THE DRUGSTORE'S LUNCH counter was to the left of the door, separated from the door by a magazine rack and the tobacco counter. She was drinking coffee at the counter, the only customer. He looked at her and, for a second or two, did not recognize her. Then he looked again and saw that it was Jill.

She looked entirely different. Her hair was a different color, a sort of medium brown, and she wore it off her face now, brought back and done up in a French twist. When she turned to him he stared. Her hair style altered the whole shape of her face.

And her face was different for other reasons, too. Her lips looked fuller, redder. Her eyes were deeper, and she seemed to be wearing a lot of makeup. She was only twenty-four but she looked a good three years older now.

He started to sputter questions but she silenced him with a finger to her lips. "Sit down," she said. "Have a cup of coffee. I'll explain it all to you."

"I think you'd better."

He sat down, and an old man with thick wire-rimmed glasses came over to take his order. He asked for coffee. He forgot to order it black, and it came with cream in it. He stirred it with a spoon. The counterman went away, and Dave waited.

She said, "I went to see Lublin."

"You must be crazy."

"No," she said. "Dave, it was the only way. We couldn't go after him until we knew what his place was like, if he lived alone or with anybody, all of that. And you couldn't go to meet him because he would have been suspicious, you never would have gotten past the door. Suppose he had live-in bodyguards. He does have one man who lives with him, as a matter of fact. If we went there without knowing it—"

"But why did *you* go?"

"Because I knew he would let me in." She drank coffee. "He wouldn't let a man in, one that he didn't know, on a night when he was having some people over. But a girl is something else again. Almost any man will open a door for a pretty girl. And let her stay as long as she wants. I told him I was supposed to meet a man there. I said—"

"What man?"

"Pete Miller. You've been using the name so much it was the first one that came to mind." She grinned quickly. "He said he didn't know any Pete Miller. I stood there looking lost and pathetic and told him I was sure that this was the address, that I was supposed to come there. I guess he de-

cided that I must be a call girl. He said it was probably somebody's idea of a joke but that I should come in out of the rain
and have a drink to warm up. It was still raining then." She
patted her hair and grinned again. "I was afraid it would
wash the color out of my hair."

He pointed to her hair. "Why?"

"Because I was afraid one of the men might be there, one
of the two men. Or anyone who might have seen the two of
us this afternoon, in case Corelli's office was watched. But
mostly because I thought Lee or the other one might be there.
I don't know if they would remember us or not, if they paid
any attention to what we looked like. I didn't want to take
chances."

"You took plenty of chances."

She sipped at her coffee again, finished it. He tried his
own. It tasted flat with cream, but at least it was hot.

She said, "After I left the hotel, I went to a drugstore, the
one where you tried to call Lublin before. I bought some
makeup and a different shade of lipstick and a color comb.
They use them to color gray hair, mostly, but it worked. I
went into a restaurant, into the rest room, and I colored my
hair and pinned it up like this. And did my lips and used
some eye shadow. Do I look very different?"

"I almost didn't recognize you."

"Like me this way?"

"Not too."

"I wanted to look different, and I also wanted to look like
a girl who might ring a man's doorbell in the middle of the
night. Do I look cheap? Not terribly cheap, but slightly
tacky?"

"Slightly tacky."

"Good. Don't worry—the makeup comes off and the hair color will wash right out. It's not a permanent transformation. Do you want to hear about Lublin?"

"Yes."

"First give me a cigarette." He gave her one, lit hers and one for himself. "Lublin lives in a house, not an apartment. A two-story house. His bedroom is upstairs, in the back. He—"

"How do you know?"

She coughed on smoke, laughing. "Are you jealous? I waited until somebody was in the bathroom downstairs and then I said I had to use the john and they sent me to the up-stairs bathroom, and I looked around upstairs. There are three bedrooms up there, one where he sleeps, one that's a television room and one set up as an office. So he sleeps up-stairs. He has a man who lives with him, sort of a bodyguard, I guess. Very muscle-bound and not bright. His name is Carl and people carry on conversations in front of him and pre-tend he isn't there. Nobody talks to him. Like the movies. He sleeps downstairs, on a daybed in the den."

"Go on."

"There were half a dozen people there, all men, plus Lub-lin and Carl. They were doing some fairly heavy drinking and talking about things that I couldn't understand. About horse racing, mostly, and other things, but nothing that I could follow. Nobody mentioned Corelli and nobody men-tioned Lee or anything. They all left by the time I did. They left first, as a matter of fact. Lublin told me, very nicely, that he would pay me a hundred dollars if I spent the night with him."

"He—"

"I told him I couldn't, that I was just supposed to meet

this Pete Miller as a favor. He didn't press." Her face was thoughtful. "He's a very pleasant man," she said quietly. "Very soft-spoken, and he tries very hard to show class. Only the most expensive brands of liquor. And very polite when he propositioned me, and very gracious when I turned him down."

There were little lines at the corners of her eyes, largely obscured by the eye shadow she wore. They were the only signs of tension he could see. Her voice was a little brittler than usual, but otherwise she spoke as calmly as though she were telling him about some mediocre film she had seen. In the hotel, he had worried about her panicking and rushing back to Binghamton because she was in over her head. He could hardly have been more wrong about her.

How little you know, he thought. How little you know about any other person. You could marry a girl and never realize what she was truly like inside, could not begin to assess her separate strengths and weaknesses. And he had never realized how very strong Jill was. He was learning.

"We can go there now," she was saying. "You have the gun, don't you?"

"Yes." It was tucked under his belt, the butt hidden by jacket and raincoat.

"I think we can take him now. Newkirk is one block over, and then he lives about a dozen blocks down Newkirk. We ought to be able to get a cab outside. This is a busy street, even at this hour. There were cabs cruising by while I was waiting for you."

"I'll go," he said.

"Don't be ridiculous. He knows me and Carl knows me. They'll open the door for me without thinking twice about it. If you went alone they would be on guard, but they already know me."

He opened his mouth automatically, to argue, and changed his mind. She was right, she had to come along. He touched the side of her face with his fingers and grinned at her. "You're one hell of a woman," he said.

"Surprised?"

"A little."

"I surprised myself," she said.

In the cab he said, "You never should have left like that. In the middle of the night without saying anything."

"I had to."

"Why?"

"Would you have let me go otherwise?"

"No. Why didn't you leave a note?"

"I didn't think you would wake up. I hoped you wouldn't. I thought about leaving a note, anyway, but I was afraid it would worry you."

"It worried me enough this way."

"I'm sorry. I thought if I left you a note you would come running straight to Lublin's, and we both would have been in trouble. It's the next block, on the left. Three houses down."

The cab pulled to a stop. They got out, and he paid the driver and told him not to wait. The cab drove off. They stood on the sidewalk and looked at Lublin's house. All the lights were off.

"They're asleep," she said.

The house was white clapboard, with a screened-in porch in front. He could see rocking chairs on the porch. A Cadillac was parked in the driveway just in front of the garage. They walked up the driveway to the side door. He reached inside his coat and pulled the revolver from under his belt. The metal of the gun was warm with his body heat. The butt fit snugly in his hand, and his finger moved to the trigger. He stood in darkness at the side of the door. She rang the bell.

"If Carl answers the door," she whispered, "let me get inside with him. Then get him from behind. He's big, he must be strong as an ox."

He could hear nothing inside the house. He nudged her, and she leaned on the doorbell, a little more insistently this time. He heard something. She poked the bell again for emphasis, and inside the house footsteps moved slowly toward them.

"Who's it?"

A voice, deep and guttural. He tensed himself in the shadows, and Jill called, "It's me, Carl. Rita. You wanna let me come in for a minute?" Her voice, he thought, was as different now as her face and her hair. Harsh and strident, with a New York inflection which sounded utterly foreign coming from her lips.

The curtains parted. He saw a face, large, heavy. A thick nose, a very broad forehead. Carl's eyes did not look at him but stayed on Jill. The doorknob turned, the door opened inward. She stepped inside.

"Whattaya want, Miss Rita?"

"Is Maurie up?"

"Sleeping. You want him?"

Dave moved softly, quickly. Carl had his back to the door now. Dave came through the door, the gun gripped by the barrel. He swung it downward with full strength, and

Carl turned toward the sound just in time to catch the butt of the gun on the side of his head instead of at the base of the skull. He blinked dizzily and Dave hit him again, across the forehead. This time he went down.

But not out. He was an ox, a hardheaded ox, and a tap on the head wasn't enough to stop him. He got to his knees and looked at Jill and at Dave. He didn't seem to notice the gun; if he saw it, he didn't pay any attention to it. He pushed himself up into a crouch and lowered his head and charged.

Dave brought up a knee that caught him in the mouth, then smashed the gun down across the broad skull once again. But Carl had momentum working for him. They both went down, with the big man on top. A table tipped and a lamp crashed down and the room went dark. The gun was still in Dave's hand but his arm was pinned to the floor. Carl was on him, too dazed to hit him, too dazed to do anything but wrestle around with his weight as a lever. He had plenty of weight to work with.

Dave heaved, tried to swing free. He drove a knee upward and caught the big man in the groin. Carl didn't seem to notice. Dave twisted, first to the left, then hard to the right. Carl was hitting him in the chest. He let go of the gun and pushed Carl's face back with both hands, then let go with his right hand and hammered at Carl's nose with the side of his palm. Blood came. Carl rolled away, holding his face with both hands. Dave hit him openhanded on the side of the throat. Carl croaked like a frog, slipped forward, fell off to the side.

The room was swaying. Dave's head ached and his mouth was dry. He didn't know where the gun was. Carl was trying to get up again, and Dave moved toward him and kicked him in the side of the head. Carl's nose was bleeding freely now. His head snapped to the side from the force of the kick. He groaned and tried again to get up but he couldn't make it. He slumped forward and lay still.

There were lights on upstairs, and sounds. A loud voice wanted to know what the hell was going on. Carl tried to get up again. Dave looked for the gun and couldn't find it. The room was lighter now with illumination from upstairs. Carl was on his knees, shaking his head and trying to clear it. Dave got the lamp, the one that had spilled from a table earlier in the fight. It was almost too heavy to lift. He picked it up and half-swung, half-dropped it on Carl. There was a thudding sound and Carl sprawled forward again and did not move.

The gun. Where in hell was the gun?

Then he heard Jill's voice, cool and clear. "You'd better come down those stairs, Maurie," he heard her say. "Come down slow and easy or I'll kill you, Maurie."

Dave turned. There was a short and plumpish man at the head of the stairs, his hands tentatively raised to shoulder height. His bathrobe, belted snugly around his thick waist, was red silk, monogrammed "ML" over the heart in flowing gold script. He had a moustache, thick and black, about an inch and a half long. His mouth was curled slightly downward at the corners. He was barefoot.

Jill stood at the foot of the stairs. Dave looked at her, then at Lublin. She was holding the gun on the little man, pointing it just as he had taught her to point it that afternoon at the doorknob in their room.

95

He walked over to her, his head still rocky. He took the gun from her hand and trained it on Lublin. Lublin came down the stairs very slowly, his hands in the air. The whole house was as silent as death.

# 9

<<<<<<<<<<<<<<<<<<<<<<<<<<<<<<<<<<<<<<<<<<<<<<<<<<<

LUBLIN STOOD at the foot of the stairs and looked at them, and at the gun. To Jill he said, "You're a damn fool, Rita. I don't keep cash around the house. Maybe a couple of hundred, no more than that."

"We're not looking for money."

"No?" He looked at Dave, eyes wary. "Then what?"

"Information."

"Then put the gun away. What kind of information?"

"About Corelli." He didn't put the gun away.

"Corelli?"

"Joe Corelli.'

"I don't know him," Lublin said. "Who is he? And put the gun away."

The man looked soft, Dave thought, except for the eyes.

There was a hardness there that didn't go with the pudgy body or the round face. "Corelli is dead," he said.

"I didn't even know he was sick."

"You had him killed."

Lublin was smiling now, with his mouth, not with his eyes. "You made a mistake somewhere," he said. "I never heard of this Corelli of yours. How could I have him killed?" He spread his hands. "You two oughta relax and go home. What do you want to point a gun at me for? You're not going to shoot me. What are you? You're a couple of kids, it's late, you ought to go home. Then—"

Dave thought, he has to believe it. He has to take it seriously, he has to feel it. But the mood wasn't right for violence. A plump little man in a bathrobe, talking easily in a calm voice. You couldn't hit him, not out of the blue.

Jill, he thought. They raped Jill. He fixed the thought very carefully in his mind, and then he stepped forward and raked the barrel of the gun across Lublin's face. Lublin looked surprised. Dave transferred the gun to his left hand and hit Lublin hard in the mouth with his right. He hit him again, in the chest, and Lublin fell back against the stairs. He sat down there, breathing heavily, holding the back of one hand to his mouth. Blood trickled from his face where the gun barrel had cut him.

"You son of a bitch," he said.

"Maybe you better start talking."

"Go to hell."

Dave said, "Do you think you can take it, old man? You didn't kill Corelli, you had it done. All I want to know is the names of the men who killed him. You're going to tell me sooner or later."

"What's Corelli to you?"

"He's nothing to me."

"Then what do you care who killed him?"

"You don't have to know."

Lublin thought this over. He got to his feet slowly, rubbing his mouth with the back of his hand. He avoided Dave's eyes, centering his gaze a foot below them. He patted the pockets of the robe and said he needed a cigarette. Dave tossed him a pack. Lublin caught the cigarettes, fumbled them, bent to scoop them from the floor. He touched the floor with one hand and came up out of the crouch, leaping for the gun. Dave kicked him in the face, stepped back, kicked him again.

They had to get water from the kitchen and throw it on him. His face was a mess. His mouth was bleeding, two teeth were gone, and one was loose. He got up and found a chair and fell into it. Dave lit a cigarette and gave it to him. Lublin took it and held it, looked at it but didn't smoke it. Dave said, "Corelli," and Lublin took a deep drag on the cigarette and coughed.

Then he said, "I knew Corelli. We had dealings now and then."

Dave didn't say anything.

"I didn't have him killed."

"The hell you didn't."

Lublin's eyes were wide. "Why would I have him hit? What did he ever do to me?"

"He owed you sixty-five thousand dollars."

"Where did you hear that?"

"From Corelli." He thought a minute, then added, "And from other people."

Dave watched his face, watched the eyes trying to de-

99

cide how to manage the lie, whether to tell none or part of the truth. And he thought suddenly of law school. Techniques in Cross-examination. They didn't teach you this, he thought. You learned how to make a witness contradict himself, how to trip him up, how to discredit testimony, all of that. But not how to worm information out of a man when you held a gun on him. They taught you how to do it with words, not how to get along when words didn't work any more.

Lublin said, "He owed me the money."

"How?"

"How? In cash."

"Why did he owe it to you?"

"A gambling debt."

"So you had him killed when he didn't pay."

"Don't be stupid," Lublin said. He was more confident now; maybe his face had stopped hurting. "He would have paid. The minute he died I was out the money. He can't pay me when he's dead."

"When did he lose the money?"

"February, March. What's the difference?"

"How?"

"Cards. He got in over his head, he borrowed, he couldn't pay back. That's all she wrote."

"What kind of game?"

"Poker."

"Poker. You let him have sixty-five thousand?"

"Fifty. Fifteen gees was interest."

He thought a minute, and Jill said, "He's lying, Dave."

"How do you know?"

"He made two-dollar race bets. You saw the slips. He wouldn't plunge like that at a card table."

Lublin said, "Listen, dammit—"

And she said, coolly, "Hit him again, Dave."

Techniques in Cross-examination. He used the barrel of the gun, raked it across the side of Maurie Lublin's face. He was careful not to knock him out this time. He just wanted to make it hurt. Lublin winced and tried to shrink back into the chair. Dave hit him again, and the cut bled lightly. It was easy now, mechanical.

"Start over," he said.

"I loaned him the money. I—"

"The truth, all the way."

"We were in on a deal."

"What kind of a deal?"

"Corelli's deal. There was a warehouse robbery in Yonkers. Instant coffee, a hijacking deal. The heavies who took the place came up with a little better than a quarter of a million dollars' worth of instant coffee. That's wholesale. When they got it, they had it set up to push it to an outfit in Detroit for a hundred thou. The thing fell in."

"So?"

"So they got in touch with Corelli. Joe handled this kind of a deal before. They didn't want to play around with the load, they just wanted their money out. He offered fifty grand for the load but they wanted better, it had to be carved up a few ways. They settled for seventy-five."

"And?"

"And Joe didn't have the seventy-five. He could raise ten but anything more was scraping, he couldn't make it. He came to me and offered me half the gross for sixty-five thousand. My capital and his connections. He had other people on the line, in Pittsburgh, to take the pile off his hands for a hundred and twenty-five thousand, which meant a gross profit of fifty thousand dollars with the whole play figured to take a little less than a month. My share would be twenty-five, and twenty-five less costs for Corelli."

"You went in with him?"

Lublin half-smiled. "For thirty, not for twenty-five. That still gave Corelli twenty thousand for his ten and nobody was going to give him a better deal. Besides, he didn't have that much time to shop around. The hijackers were in a hurry. He took my sixty-five and his ten and bought them out. That gave us half the coffee in the world, and Joe had the place to move it, to Pittsburgh."

"What happened?"

"The rest made the papers. This was in March. Corelli hired a trucker. The trucker stopped to make time with a waitress, and the other trucks with him got ahead of him, and this one schmuck got nervous and started speeding to catch up. On the Pennsy Turnpike, in a truck, the son of a bitch is speeding. One of those long-distance trucks and they never speed, they always hold it steady." He shook his head, still angry with the driver. "So a trooper stopped him and this driver got nervous, and the trooper got suspicious, and the driver pulls a gun and the trooper shoots his head off, like that. They opened the truck and found a load of hot coffee, and they radioed ahead and cut off the other trucks, and that was the shipment, all of it, with the drivers off to jail and the coffee back to the warehouse where it came from in the first place."

"And you were out the money?"

"We weren't exactly insured."

"But why did Corelli owe you the dough?"

"Because it was his fault the deal fell in," Lublin said. "It was his play. I was investing, and he was supposed to manage it. He was responsible for delivering the load and collecting payment. All I had going was my capital. When it fell in, he owed me my cost, which was sixty-five thousand." He narrowed his eyes slightly. He said, "I knew he didn't have it then, because if he had had it he would have carried the deal all by himself, he wouldn't have cut me in. It wasn't the kind of debt where I was going to press him for payment. He didn't have it, and the hell, you don't get blood from a stone. But he would get it, little by little. He would pay up, and I had no instant need for the money. When he got it he would pay me. In the meanwhile, he owed me. If I needed a favor I could go to him because he owed me. Joe was small but not so small it hurt me to have him owe me favors. That never hurts, it can always be handy."

"Then why have him killed?"

"I didn't. That's the whole point, why I wouldn't be the one to have him killed. There was nothing personal. It was his fault the deal went sour, sure, but that was nothing personal. And killing him could only cost money without getting any money back. Use your head, why would I kill him?"

"Then who did?"

"I don't know."

"But you have ideas."

"No ideas," Lublin said.

"He was out his own ten thousand dollars and he owed

you sixty-five thousand on top of it. He must have been hungry for big money, and fast. What was he doing?"

"He didn't tell me."

"Who was he involved with?"

"I don't know."

"He mentioned your name when they went to kill him. He said to tell you he would pay up the money, but they shot him anyway."

"You were there?"

Maybe it was a mistake to let him know that, he thought. The same mistake as Jill's mentioning his name. The hell with it.

"He mentioned your name," he said again. "He thought you were the one who had him killed."

"I don't get it. Where do you and the broad come in?"

"We come in right here. Corelli thought you killed him. Why should I think any different?"

"I told you—"

"I know what you told me. Now you have to tell me something else. You have to tell me who had him killed, because that's something you would know, it's something you would have to know. Corelli left town three months ago, running for his life. He owed you a pile of money. If anybody owed you that kind of money and skipped town you would know why. He was either running from you or running from somebody else, and either way you would damn well know about it."

Lublin didn't say anything.

"You're going to tell me. I've got the gun, and your man over there isn't going to be any help to you, and I don't care what kind of a job I have to do on you to get you to talk. I'll take you apart if I have to. I mean that."

"How did you get so hard?" Dave looked at him. "You talk too clean, you look too clean. You don't come on like a hotster. But you got guts like a hotster. Who the hell are you?"

"Nobody you know. Who was Corelli running from?"

"Maybe his shadow."

A slap this time, openhanded across the face. Lublin's head snapped back from the blow, and he said something dirty. The back of the hand this time, again across the face, the head snapping back once again, the face flushed where the slaps had landed. Techniques in Cross-examination.

Dave said, "I don't care who had him killed, whether it was you or somebody else. I'm not looking for the man who gave the order."

"Then—"

"I'm looking for the two men who did the killing."

"The guns?"

"Yes."

"Why?"

He didn't answer. Lublin looked at him, then at Jill, then said, "I don't get it."

"You don't have to."

"You want to know the names of the two men who took Corelli and shot him. The ones hired to hit him."

"Yes."

"Well, I don't know that."

"You don't?"

"If I had him killed," Lublin said guardedly, "even then

I wouldn't know the actual names of the guns. I would call someone, a friend, and say that there was this Corelli and I wanted him found and killed, and I would pay so much dough to this friend, and that's all I would know. He might fly a couple of boys all the way in from the West Coast, and they would do the job, make the hit, and then they would be on the next plane back to S.F. or somewhere. Or even local boys, I wouldn't know their names or who they were."

"Then tell me who you called."

"I didn't call anybody. I was just saying that even if I did I still wouldn't know the guns."

"Then tell me who did make the call. Who had Corelli killed?"

"I told you. I don't know that."

"I think you do."

"Dammit—"

Monotonous Techniques in Cross-examination. It took a long time, a batch of questions, a stone wall of silence, a barrage of pistol-whipping and slapping, a gun butt laid across Lublin's knee, the barrel of the gun slapped against the side of his jaw. There would be a round of beating, and a round of unanswered questions, and another round of beating.

Jill hardly seemed to be there at all. She stood silent, cigarette now and then, went away once to use the bathroom. Carl never moved and never made a sound. He lay inert on the far side of the room and nobody ever went over to look at him. There was Lublin in the chair and there was Dave with the gun, standing over him, and they went around and around that way.

Until Lublin said, "You'll kill me. I'm not so young, I'll have a heart attack. Jesus, you'll kill me."

"Then talk."

"I swear I did not have him hit. I swear to God I did not have that man hit."

"Then tell me who did."

"I can't tell you."

"You know who it was."

"I know but I can't say."

Progress. "You don't have any choice. You have to say, Lublin."

He did not hit him this time, did not even draw the gun back. Lublin sat for a long moment, thinking. Outside, it was light already. Daylight came in around the edges of the drapes. Maybe Lublin was trying to stall, maybe he thought he could take punishment until somebody showed up. But he was running out of gas. No one had come and he couldn't take it any more.

"If they find out I told you," he said, "then I'm dead."

"They won't find out. And you'll be just as dead if you don't talk."

He didn't seem to have heard. In a dull dead voice he said, "Corelli wanted money fast. He owed other people beside me but nothing big, not to anybody else. He was strapped for capital. He couldn't make fast money legit because his construction operation was down to nothing but the office and the name. He was mostly a middleman anyway and everything he had owned before was tied up now or cleared out. He stripped himself pretty badly getting up the ten grand for the instant-coffee deal."

"Keep talking."

"He did a stupid thing. He was stuck and he was up against it, and he knew I wasn't going to wait forever for the sixty-five thou, not forever, and he needed maybe a hundred grand or better to be completely out from under and able to operate. He got a smart idea, he was going to middleman a hundred grand worth of heroin to someone with a use for it. You understand what I mean?"

"Yes. Where did he get the heroin?"

"He never had it. That was the stupid idea. He was going to sell it without having it, get the money and deliver something else, face powder, anything. It was stupid and he would have gotten himself killed even if he pulled it off, but he maybe figured that with a hundred grand he could get into something good and double the money and pay back before his man tipped to the play, and then he would be back in the clear. It was risky as hell and it didn't stand a chance. He was sure to get himself killed that way."

"What happened?"

"The man he was dealing with—"

"Who was he?"

Lublin tensed.

"You'll tell me anyway. Make it easy on yourself."

"Jesus. It was Washburn. You know him?"

"No. His first name?"

"Ray. Ray Washburn."

"Where does he live?"

"I don't know. Up in the Bronx."

He's lying, he thought. He said, "You've got an address book in the house. Where is it?"

"An address book—"

"Yes. Where is it?"

Lublin was defeated. He said it was upstairs, in the den, and Jill went up for it. He looked under "W" and found a

Frank Washburn listed, with a Manhattan address and a telephone number. He said, "You must have gotten the name wrong. It's Frank Washburn, and he lives in Manhattan. That's right, isn't it?"

Lublin didn't answer.

"All right. He went to Washburn. What happened?"

"Washburn said he would let him know. He checked around, and he found out that Corelli was in hock up to his ears and he couldn't have the stuff, that it had to be a con. He didn't let on that he knew, just told Joe he wasn't interested, that he couldn't use the stuff. Joe dropped the price still further and Washburn knew it had to be a con then, it couldn't be anything else at that price, so he just kept on saying he wasn't interested.

"But the word got around, about what Joe had tried to pull, and Washburn saw it was bad to let him get away with it, if people tried to con him like that and got by with it, he would get a bad name. And he was mad, anyway, because he is not the type of man people set up for stupid con games and Joe should have known this. So he marked Joe for a hit."

"Who did he hire?"

"I don't know. If I knew that I would give it to you. I would give it a long time before I would give you Washburn."

"Why didn't Corelli know it was Washburn who was after him? Why did he think it was you?"

"Because Washburn turned the deal down. Corelli didn't know Washburn had it in for him. He thought he just turned the deal down because he had no use for the goods."

"Then why did he get out of town?"

"Because Washburn sent somebody to make a hit, and

Corelli was shot at but the gun missed, and he knew some-body was trying to kill him, and he must have figured it was me because I was the one he owed heavy money to. When somebody's shooting at you, you don't look to see the serial number on the gun. You get the hell out of town."

Dave looked over at Jill. She was nodding thoughtfully. It all made sense. He nodded himself. He looked down at Lublin now and he said, "You're not calling Washburn. You don't want to warn him."

Lublin looked up.

"You took a hell of a beating to keep from giving me his name," Dave went on. "You don't want him to know you talked to me. He won't find out from me. If he finds out, it'll be from you. You know what he'll do to you if he finds out, so you don't want to tell him."

"I won't call him."

"Good."

"Because I'll get you myself," Lublin said. "It may be fast and it may be slow, you son of a bitch, but it is damned well going to happen." A hand wiped blood from his mouth. "You are going to catch it, you and your pig of a broad. You bet-ter get to Washburn very fast, kid, or you won't get to him at all. Because there's going to be a whole army with noth-ing to do but kill you."

Dave knocked him out. He took him out easily, not angry, not wanting to hurt him, just anxious to put him on ice for the time being. He did it with the gun butt just behind the ear and Lublin did not even try to dodge the blow, did not even shrink from it. Lublin took it, and went back and out, and when Dave poked him he didn't move.

An army, Lublin had said.

But the army would not include Carl. They checked him before they left and he was still out, all that time, so they checked a little more closely. They saw that the last blow, with the lamp, had caved in the side of his skull. He was dead.

# 10

<<<<<<<<<<<<<<<<<<<<<<<<<<<<<<<<<<<<<<<<<<<<<<<<<<<<<<<<<<<<

THE DINER HAD no jukebox. Behind the counter a radio
blared. The song was an old one, Ella Fitzgerald and Louis
Jordan doing "Stone Cold Dead in the Market." The air was
thick with cooking smells. The diner had two booths, and
both of them had been occupied when they entered it. They
had adjoining seats at the counter. He was drinking coffee
and waiting for the counterman to finish making him a bowl
of oatmeal. She had coffee too and was eating a toasted English muffin. His cigarette burned slowly in a glass ashtray.
She was not smoking.

The diner was on Broadway just below Union Square.
When they left Lublin's house, they had walked along Newkirk Avenue as far as Fifteenth, and there was a subway entrance there. They went downstairs and bought tokens and

passed through the turnstile and waited in silence for a Manhattan-bound train. The train came after a long wait—the BMT Brighton line, just a few cars at that hour, just a very few passengers. They rode it as far as Fourteenth Street and got out there. From the subway arcade, the diner looked like as good a place as they would be likely to find there. It was around seven when they went into the diner. They had been there for about twenty minutes.

A man who had been sitting next to Jill folded his copy of the *Times* and left the diner. Dave leaned closer to her and said, "I killed him." She stared down into her coffee cup and didn't answer. "I murdered a man," he said.

"Not murder. It was self-defense. You were fighting and—"

He shook his head. "If an individual dies in the course of or as a direct result of the commission of a felony, the felon is guilty of murder in the first degree."

"Did we commit a felony?"

"A batch of them. Illegal entry as a starter, and a few different kinds of aggravated assault. And Carl is dead. That means that I'm guilty of first-degree murder and you're an accessory."

"Will anything—"

"Happen to us? No." He paused. "The law won't do anything. They won't hear about it, not officially at least. I understand there's a standard procedure in cases like this. Lublin will get rid of Carl's body."

"The river?"

"I don't know how they do it nowadays. I read something about putting them under roadbeds. You know—they have a friend doing highway construction, and they shovel the body into the roadbed during the night and cover him up the next day, and he's buried forever. I read somewhere that there are more than twenty dead men under the New Jersey Turnpike. The cars roll right over them and never know it."

"God," she said.

His oatmeal came, finally, a congealed mass in the bottom of the bowl. He spooned a little sugar onto it and poured some milk over the mass. He got a little of it down and gave up, pushed the bowl away. The counterman asked if anything was wrong with it and he said no, he just wasn't as hungry as he had thought. He ordered more coffee. The coffee, surprisingly, was very good there.

He said, "We're in trouble, you know."

"From Lublin?"

"Yes. He wasn't just talking. For one thing, we shoved him around pretty hard. He's a tough old man and he took it well but I hurt him, I know that. I messed him up and I hurt him. He's not going to write that off too easily. But more than that, I managed to get Washburn's name out of him, and the whole story of why Corelli was killed. He took a hell of a beating to keep from giving me Washburn's name. He won't want Washburn to find out that he let it out, and he'll be sure that Washburn will find out if we get to him. So he'll want to get us first. To have us killed."

"Will he be able to find us?"

"Maybe." He thought. "He knows my first name. You called me Dave in front of him."

"It was a slip. Does he still think my name is Rita?"

"I don't know. Maybe."

"I don't want to be killed." She said this very calmly and levelly, as though she had considered the matter very care-

fully before coming to the conclusion that death was something to be avoided if at all possible. "I don't want him to
kill us."

"It won't happen."

"He knows your first name, and he's got my name wrong.
That's all he knows, and a description of us. But the description doesn't have to fit, does it? Do you think it's time for me
to be a blonde again?"

"That's not a bad idea."

"Pay the check," she said. "I'll meet you outside, around
the corner."

He finished his coffee and paid the check. She got up and
went to the washroom in the back. He left a tip and went
outside. The sky was clear now, and the sun was bright. He
lit a cigarette. The smoke was strong in his lungs. Too many
cigarettes, too long a time without sleep. He took another
drag on the cigarette and walked to the corner of Thirteenth
Street. He finished the cigarette and tossed it into the gutter.

When she came to him he stared hard at her. The transformation was phenomenal. She was his Jill again, the hair
blond with just a trace of the brown coloring still remaining.
She had undone the French twist and the hair was pageboy
again, framing her face as it had always done. Her face was
scrubbed free of the heavy makeup. She had even removed
her lipstick and had replaced it with her regular shade. And,
with the transformation, her face had lost its hard angular
quality, had softened visibly. She had played the role of
cheap chippy so effectively that the performance had very
nearly sold him; he had almost grown used to her that way.
**It was jarring to see her again as she had always been before.**

"I didn't do a very good job," she said. "I didn't want to soak my hair, and I couldn't get all the brown out. I'll take care of it later, but this ought to do for now. How do I look?"

He told her.

"But it was fun pretending," she said. "I liked being Rita, just for a while. I must be a frustrated actress."

"Or a frustrated prostitute."

"Frustrated."

"Jill, I'm sorry."

"Don't be silly."

"I was teasing, I didn't think—"

"It's my fault. We ought to be able to tease each other."

"It was tactless."

"We should not have to be tactful with each other. Let's forget it. What do you want to do now?"

"I don't know."

"Where should we go?"

"We could go back to the hotel," he said. "You must be exhausted."

"Not especially."

"You didn't sleep at all. And you didn't sleep very well the night before last, either. Aren't you tired?"

"Very, but not sleepy. I don't think I could sleep. Are you tired?"

"No."

"Do you want to go back to the hotel?"

"No." He lit another cigarette. She took it from him and dragged on it. He told her to keep it and lit another for himself. He said, "I think we ought to find out a little about Washburn. If he's so important he probably made the papers at one time or another. We could spend an hour at the library. They keep the *New York Times* on microfilm, and it's indexed. It might be worth an hour."

"All right. Do you know how to get there? The library?"

He had used it once before, during the course for the bar exam, and he remembered where it was. They couldn't get a cab. The morning rush hour had started and there were no cabs. They walked along Thirteenth Street to catch a bus heading uptown.

He said, "You know, with Carl dead, that's one less person who knows what we look like. Lublin is the only one who can identify us."

"You're upset, aren't you?"

He looked at her.

"About Carl," she said.

"That I killed him?"

"Yes."

"Partly," he said. He threw his cigarette away. "And I'm partly upset that I didn't kill Lublin. I should have."

"You couldn't do that," she said.

"All I had to do was hit him a little too hard. Later I could tell myself I didn't mean to kill him, that it was just miscalculation on my part or weakness on his. And we wouldn't have anyone after us, we would be in the clear. It would have been logical enough."

"But you couldn't do it, Dave."

"I guess not," he said.

Francis James Washburn had appeared in the *Times* almost a dozen times in the course of the past five years. Twice he had been called to Washington to testify before senatorial investigating committees, once in a study of gangland control of boxing, once in an investigation of labor racketeering. In each instance he had pleaded the Fifth Amendment, refusing to answer any and all questions on the grounds that he might incriminate himself. The questions themselves suggested that Washburn had some hidden connections with a local of a building-trade-workers' union, that he was unofficial president of a local of restaurant and hotel employees, that he owned a principal interest in a welterweight named Little Kid Morton, and that he was otherwise fundamentally involved in the subjects of the senatorial investigations to a considerable degree.

He had been arrested three times. He was charged with conspiracy in a bribery case involving a municipal official. He was charged with suspicion of possession of narcotics. He was picked up in a raid on a floating crap game and was then charged with vagrancy and with being a common gambler. Each time the charges were dropped for lack of evidence and Washburn was released. In one of the stories, the *Times* reported that Washburn had served two years in prison during the Second World War, having been convicted for receiving stolen goods. He had also done time during the thirties for assault and battery, and had been acquitted of manslaughter charges in 1937.

His other mentions in the newspaper were minor ones. He was listed as a major contributor to the campaign fund of a Republican member of the New York State Assembly. He was among those attending a Tammany Hall fund-raising dinner. He was a pallbearer at another politician's funeral.

The over-all picture that emerged was one of a man fifty-five or sixty years old, one who had started in the lower echelons of the rackets and who had done well, moving up the ladder to a position bordering upon unholy respectability. Washburn had a great many business interests and a great many political connections. He was important and he was successful. He would be harder to reach than Maurice Lublin.

They spent a little more than an hour in the library's microfilm room. When they got back to the hotel, the night clerk was gone and another man was behind the desk. They went upstairs. They showered, and Jill rinsed the remaining coloring out of her hair and combed and set it. Dave put on a summer suit. Jill wore a skirt and blouse. They were in the room for about an hour, then went downstairs and left the hotel.

Washburn lived at 47 Gramercy Park East. They didn't know where that was, and Dave ducked into a drugstore and looked up the address in a street guide. It was on the East Side, around Twentieth Street between Third and Fourth Avenues.

They took a cab and got off three blocks away at the corner of East Seventeenth Street and Irving Place. They were only a few blocks from the diner where they had had breakfast. The neighborhood was shabby-genteel middle class, unimpressively respectable. The buildings were mostly brownstones. There were trees, but not many of them. The neighborhood picked up as they walked north on Irving Place.

He wondered if Lublin had Washburn's place staked out. It was possible, he thought. He reached under his jacket and felt the weight of the gun tucked beneath his belt. They kept walking.

# *11*

◀◀◀◀◀◀◀◀◀◀◀◀◀◀◀◀◀◀◀◀◀◀◀◀◀◀◀◀◀◀◀◀◀◀◀◀◀◀◀◀◀◀◀◀◀◀◀◀

THE BUILDING at 47 Gramercy Park East was a large four-story brownstone that had been thoroughly renovated around the end of the war. There were four apartments, one to a floor. There was a doorman in front, a tall Negro wearing a maroon uniform with gold piping. No, the doorman told Jill, there was no Mr. Watson in the building, but there was a Mr. Washburn up on the fourth floor, if that was who she wanted. She said it wasn't and he smiled a servile smile.

So Washburn was on the fourth floor. They crossed the street and moved halfway down the block, out of range of the doorman. The green square of park was bordered on all sides by a high iron fence. There was a gate, locked. A neat metal sign indicated that if you lived in one of the buildings surrounding the park you were given a key to that gate, and then you were allowed to go into the park when you wanted. Otherwise the park was out of bounds. They stood near the gate and Dave smoked a cigarette.

Jill said, "We can't stand here forever. Lublin will send somebody around sooner or later."

"Or the police will pick us up for loitering."

"Uh-huh. What do we do? Can we go up there after him?"

"No. He wouldn't be alone. One of the newspaper stories mentioned a wife, so she would be there with him, I suppose. And he probably has plenty of help. Bodyguards, a maid, all of that."

"Then what do we do?"

"I don't know," he said.

They walked to the corner. A uniformed policeman passed them, heading downtown. He didn't smile. They stood on the corner while the light changed twice.

"If we could get into the park—" he said.

"We don't have a key."

"I know," he said. "From the park, we could keep an eye on the doorway without being seen. It would be natural enough. We could sit on a bench and wait for something to happen. We don't even know if Washburn's home, or who's with him. Or what he looks like, for that matter. The one picture in the paper wasn't much good. Blurred, the way news photos always are—"

"All those little dots."

"And not a close-up anyway. We might be able to see him, he might come out alone, we could have a crack at following him. He's the key to it. Unless Lublin was doing an awfully good job of last-minute lying, Washburn is our only connection with the killers."

"Do you think we could get him to talk?"

"I don't know. For a while I didn't think Lublin would talk." He looked over at Washburn's building. "The damn thing would have to face a park," he said. "In the movies, they always rent an apartment right across the street from the suspect and set themselves up with binoculars and gun-shot microphones and tape recorders and everything else in the world, and they've got him cold. But what the hell do you do when the son of a bitch lives across from a park that you can't even get into?"

"Maybe next door?"

The buildings on either side of Washburn's were more of the same, renovated brownstones with an air of monied respectability about them. There would be no rooms for rent there, he thought. Not at all. But maybe around in back . . . "Come on," he said.

A Fourth Avenue office building was around the block from Washburn's brownstone. They looked at the building directory in the lobby. There were three lawyers, two CPA's, one insurance agency, one employment agency, a commercial-art studio, and a handful of small businesses identified in such a way that they might have done anything from advertising layout to import-export. The elevator seemed to be out of order. They walked up steep stairs to the fourth floor. The whole rear wall of the floor was taken up by one business, an outfit called Beadle & Graber. The office door was shut and the window glass frosted. A typewriter made frantic sounds behind the closed door.

He went to the door and knocked on it. The typewriter stopped quickly and a gray-haired woman opened the door cautiously. Dave asked if a Mr. Floyd Harper worked there, and the gray-haired woman said no, there was no Mr. Harper there. He looked over her shoulder at the window. It faced out upon a courtyard, and across the courtyard he could see the rear windows of Washburn's apartment. The drapes were open, but he didn't have time to see much of anything. But if he were closer to the windows, and if he had a pair of binoculars—

"You can see Washburn's apartment from their window," he told Jill.

"Then it's a shame they have the office. If it were vacant, we could rent it."

"There's still a way."

"How?"

"Wait for me in the lobby," he said.

They walked as far as the third floor together. Then she went on downstairs while he knocked on the door of one of the CPA's. A voice told him to come in. He went inside. A balding man in his forties asked what he could do for him.

Dave said, "Just wanted to ask a question, if I could. I was thinking of taking an office in this building. There's space available, isn't there?"

"I think so. On the top floor, I believe."

"Just one thing I wanted to know. Is this a twenty-four-hour building? Can you get in and out any time?"

You could, the accountant told him. They kept a night man on duty to run the elevator, and from six at night until eight in the morning you had to sign a register if you entered or left the building. "It's not a bad location," the accountant said. "The address has a little more prestige than it used to. It's Park Avenue South now, not Fourth Avenue. Everybody in the city still calls it Fourth Avenue, of course, but it gives you a more impressive letterhead, at least for the out-of-town people. You want the rental agent's phone number?"

"I've already got it," Dave said.

There was a coffee shop two doors down the street, empty now in the gap between breakfast and lunch crowds. They ate at odd times lately, he thought. They settled in one of the empty booths and ordered sliced-chicken sandwiches. She had coffee, he had milk. The sandwiches were good and he was hungrier than he had thought. And tired, suddenly. He didn't want to sleep, but he felt the physical need for it. A couple of times he caught himself staring dully ahead, his mind neatly empty, as if it had temporarily turned itself off. He ordered coffee after all and forced himself to drink it.

"I can go back there during the night," he told her. He explained the way the building was kept open. "I can sign some name to the book and break into that office."

"Break into it?"

"Pick the lock. Or break the window and unlock it. There won't be anybody around, and once I'm in I can get a good look into his place. Washburn's." But then he stopped and shook his head. "No," he said. "That's crazy, isn't it?"

"It sounds risky. If anybody heard you—"

"More than that. In the first place, he probably closes his drapes when it gets dark out. Everybody does. Besides, all I could see would be the one room of the apartment, and it's probably a bedroom anyway. I couldn't keep an eye on the front door, and I would never know if he left the building. We have to be able to see the front of his building, not the back of it."

*Deadly Honeymoon*

A few minutes later she looked up and said, "But there is something we can do, honey."

"What?"

"Instead of breaking into the office. Or sneaking in. And it should be easier, and less dangerous. We could break into Gramercy Park."

They waited on the north side of the park, about twenty yards down from the main gate. The privilege of a key to the park was evidently more symbolic than utilitarian. The park was empty except for a very old man who wore a black suit and a maroon bow tie and who sat reading the *Wall Street Journal* and moving his lips as he read. They waited for him to leave the park but he seemed determined to sit on his bench forever. They waited a full half hour before anyone else entered the park. Then a woman came, a very neat and very old woman in a gray tweed suit. She had a cairn terrier on a braided leather leash. She opened the gate with a key and led the dog inside and they watched the gate swing shut behind her.

The woman spent twenty minutes in the park, leading the cairn from one tree to another. The small dog seemed to have an extraordinary capacity for urine. They completed the tour, finally, and woman and dog headed for the gate. Their move was well timed. The two of them reached the gate just as the woman was struggling with the lock. She opened it, and Dave drew the gate open while Jill made a show of admiring the dog. The dog admired them. The woman and the dog passed through the gate, and Jill stepped inside and Dave started to follow her.

The woman said, "You have your own key, of course."

"I left it in the apartment," Jill said. She smiled disarmingly. "We're right across the street." She pointed vaguely toward Washburn's building.

The woman looked at them, her eyes bright. "No," she said gently, "I don't think you are."

The dog tugged at the leash but the woman stood her ground. "One so rarely sees younger people at this park," she said. "Isn't it barbaric, taking something as lovely as a park and throwing a fence around it? The world has too many fences and too few parks. There are times when I think Duncan"—she nodded at the dog—"has the only proper attitude toward this fence. He occasionally employs it as a substitute tree. You don't live in this neighborhood, do you?"

"Well—"

"You sound as though you're from upstate somewhere. Not native New Yorkers, certainly." She shook her head. "Such intrigue just to rest a moment in a pleasant park. You're married, of course. Wearing a wedding ring, both of you are, and the rings seem to match. And even if they didn't I'd be good enough to give you the benefit of the doubt and assume that you're married to each other. From out of town, and anxious to sit together in a park—" The woman smiled pleasantly. "Probably on a honeymoon," she said. "After a year or two of marriage you'll have had your fill of parks, I'm sure. And, probably, of each other."

"Oh, I hope not," Jill said.

The woman's smile spread. "So do I, my dear, so do I. You're quite welcome to the park. My late husband and I used to go to Washington Square when we were courting. Isn't that a dated term? I'm old, aren't I?"

"I don't think so."

"You're very charming, aren't you? But I very certainly am old, nevertheless. Courting. I understand Washington Square's changed a great deal since then. A great many young persons with leather jackets and beards and guitars. Perhaps that's an argument for gates and fences after all. Every question has so many sides. I am a silly old woman, aren't I?"

"No."

"Enjoy the park," the woman said, passing through the gate now. "And enjoy each other. And don't grow old too quickly, if you'll pardon more advice. Giving unwanted advice is one of the few remaining privileges of the aged, you know. Don't grow old too quickly. Being old is not really very much fun. It's better than being dead, but that's really about all one can say for it."

The iron gate swung shut. The woman and the dog walked quickly with small and precise steps to the corner and waited for the signal to change. Then they crossed the street and continued down the block.

"We really fooled her," Jill said.

"Uh-huh."

They went to a bench on a path running along the western edge of the park. They were almost directly across from Washburn's apartment house. The same doorman still stood at the door.

"We did fool her," Jill said suddenly.

"That woman? How?"

"She thought we were a nice young couple," Jill said. "I guess we used to be." She looked away. "I'm not sure we are now," she said quietly.

# *12*

<<<<<<<<<<<<<<<<<<<<<<<<<<<<<<<<<<<<<<<<<<<<<<<<<<<

THEIR BENCH was shaded by two tall elms. There, in the park, the air was cleaner and cooler than in the surrounding city. They sat close together on the bench, looking over a stretch of green and through the grating of the fence at the luxury apartment buildings across the small street. The setting did not match the circumstances at all. Too placid, too secure. His mind would wander, and he had to force himself to remember what they were there for, and why. Otherwise he kept relaxing to fit the old woman's image. A couple of honeymooners who wanted a few peaceful moments for themselves away from the hot hurry of New York.

Other images helped him concentrate. The five bullets pumped one after another into Joe Corelli's head. The professionally disinterested beating he himself had taken. The direct and dispassionate rape of Jill. The cold fury of the ride into the city. Carl, Lublin's personal heavyweight, first lumbering like a gored ox, then dead.

The watching was hard. It had seemed direct enough at the beginning, a stakeout straight out of *Dragnet*. You took a position and you held it and you waited for something to happen. But there was one basic difficulty. Nothing happened.

No one left Washburn's building and no one entered it. The doorman stood at his post. At one point he lit a cigar, and after about twenty minutes he threw the cigar into the gutter. Cars drove by, the traffic never very thick. Occasionally someone with a key came into the park, either to walk a leashed dog or to sit reading a book or an afternoon paper. The drapes were still open in Frank Washburn's apartment but it was on the fourth floor, and they were at ground level. They could tell that there were lights on, which meant there was probably someone at home, but that was all they could tell.

So it became hard to concentrate. They talked, but concentration had an unreal quality to it. There wasn't much to say about the job at hand, about Washburn and where he might lead them. Once they had gone over that a few times they were tired of it. And any other conversation was fairly well out of place. Mostly, they sat together in silence. The silence would be broken now and then—she would ask for a cigarette, or one of them would ask a question that the other would quickly answer. Then the silence would come back again.

Until she said, "That car was here before."

He looked up quickly. She was nodding toward a metallic-gray Pontiac that was turning west at the corner of Twentieth Street. He caught a quick look at it before another car blocked his view.

"Are you sure?"

"Yes. About five minutes ago. This time it just coasted by slowly, as if they were looking for somebody."

"Like us?"

"Maybe."

"Did you—"

"I think there were two people in the car. I'm not sure. The first time, I didn't pay much attention. Who looks at cars? Then the second time, just after they passed us, I remembered the car. There's a spotlight mounted on the hood. That's what I noticed that made me remember the car. You don't see that many of them."

"And the men?"

"I'm not even sure they were both men. The driver was. By the time I realized that it was the same car they had already passed us and all I saw were the backs of their heads."

His hand went automatically to the gun, secure under the waistband of his slacks. He patted the gun almost affectionately, a nervous gesture. We are getting close now, he thought. Before we were looking for them, and now people are looking for us.

"I wish you'd had a better look at them."

"Maybe they'll be back."

"Yes." He started to light a cigarette, then changed his mind. Get up and get out, he thought. They could see into the park. This next time, they might get lucky and spot them. And then—

No, they had to stay where they were. If they could get a

look at the men in the Pontiac, they were that much ahead of the game. They could not afford the luxury of running scared.

"Lublin must have sent them," he said.

"I suppose so."

"It only stands to reason. He doesn't want Washburn to know that he talked, and he knows we're going to try to get information from Washburn. So he would have Washburn's place watched and try to head us off on the way there. It evidently took him a little while to get organized. That was good luck for us. Otherwise they would have seen us wandering around the street and—"

It was a good sentence to leave unfinished. He reached again for a cigarette, the movement an instinctive one, and his hand stopped halfway to his breast pocket. He said, "That means Washburn doesn't know."

"You mean about us?"

"Yes. If he knew, he would have men outside, waiting for us. But if Lublin didn't tell him, then Lublin would have to accomplish two things. He would have to keep us from getting to Washburn, and at the same time he would have to watch the place without arousing suspicion. He would want to get to us without Washburn knowing anything about the whole play. Where are you going?"

She was standing, walking toward the fence. "To see better," she said. "In case that car comes back."

He grabbed her hand and pulled her back. "Don't be a damned fool. We can see them well enough from farther back. And we can't risk having them see us."

He led her back across a cement walk and sat down with her on another bench. There was an extra screening of shrubbery now between them and the street. They could see through it, but it would be hard for anyone passing by to get a good look at them.

"It might not have been anything," he said.

"The Pontiac?"

"It could have been somebody driving around the block and looking for a place to park. You sort of coast along like that when you're trying to find a parking place."

"Maybe, but—"

"But what?"

"I don't know. Just a feeling."

And he had the same feeling. It was funny, too—he half-wanted the car to turn out to be innocent, because the idea of being pursued while pursuing added a new and dangerous element to the situation. But at the same time pursuit now would be a good sign. It would mean Washburn didn't know what was happening, which was good. It would mean for certain that Lublin's story was true.

A few minutes later he saw the Pontiac again. Jill nudged him and pointed but he had already noticed the car himself. It was coming from the opposite direction this time, cruising uptown past Washburn's apartment toward Twenty-first Street. It was a four-door car, the windows rolled down, the back seat empty. It was going between fifteen and twenty miles an hour.

There were two men in the front seat. At first he couldn't get a good look at them. He squinted, and as the car drew up even with them he got a good look at the man on the passenger side. He drew in his breath sharply, and he felt Jill's hand on his arm, her fingers tightening, squeezing hard.

Then as the car moved off he got a brief glimpse of the man behind the wheel.

The man on the passenger side was thickset and short-necked with a heavy face and a once-broken nose. The man doing the driving had thick eyebrows and a thin mouth and a scattering of thin hairline scars across the bridge of his nose.

The car was gone now. It had turned at the corner, had continued west at Twenty-first Street, picking up speed once it rounded the corner. He looked after it and watched it disappear quickly from view. He turned to Jill. She had let go of his arm, and both of her hands were in her lap, knotted into tight fists. Her face was a blend of hatred and horror.

Lee and his friend. Corelli's murderers. Their target.

They got out of there in a hurry. He said her name and she blinked at him as though her mind were elsewhere, caught up either in the memory of violation or in the plans for vengeance. He said, "Come on, we've got to take off." She got to her feet and they let themselves out of the park and walked off in the opposite direction, toward Third Avenue. An empty cab came by and they grabbed it. He told the driver to take them to the Royalton.

They started uptown on Third. Jill said, "Suppose they know about the hotel?"

"How?"

"I don't know. I'm just panicky, I guess."

"They might know," he said. He leaned forward. "Just leave us at the corner of Thirty-fourth Street," he said.

"Not the Royalton?"

"No, just on the corner."

"Thirty-fourth and where?"

"And Third," he said.

There was a bar on Third halfway between Thirty-fourth and Thirty-fifth. They got out of the cab and walked to it. He didn't relax until they were inside the bar and seated in a booth in the rear. It was ridiculous, he knew. The Pontiac was nowhere near them, they were safe, they were clear. But he couldn't walk in the open street without the uncomfortable feeling that someone was watching them.

There was no waitress. He went to the bar and got two bottles of Budweiser and two glasses, paid for the beers and carried them to the booth. He poured beer into his glass and took a drink. She let her beer sit untouched on the table in front of her. She opened her mouth as if to speak, then shook her head suddenly and closed her mouth again without saying anything.

Finally she said, "I don't understand it."

"What?"

"Lublin didn't know who the killers were. That's what he said, isn't it?"

"Yes."

"Then he must have been lying. Lee and the other man were in the car. They were driving around looking for us. Is there anyone besides Lublin who knows about us?"

"No. Unless someone recognized you at Lublin's last night."

"Who? No one could have. So Lublin had to tell them. That meant that he hired them in the first place, and that the whole business about Washburn was a lot of nonsense, and that—"

"He wasn't lying."

"He must have been. He—"

"No. Wait a minute." He picked up the glass of beer and took a long drink. The beer was very cold and went down easily. He made rings on the top of the table with the cold glass.

He said, "Lublin was telling the truth. I think I see it now. After we left, there were two things he had to do. He had to keep us from getting to Washburn, first of all. But he also had to let Lee and the other one know about us, that we were coming. They were the logical people to set after us. They were the ones we were after, first of all, and that would give them a personal stake in nailing us. It would save his hiring men to run us down, too. All he had to do was tell the two of them that a man and a woman were in town looking for Corelli's killers, and then the two of them would handle the rest. If they got to us and killed us, Lublin was in the clear. And if we got to them first, and killed them, he was still in the clear. Because we would pack up and move out without Washburn hearing about the whole deal."

"Is he really that scared of Washburn?"

"Washburn killed Corelli—had him killed, that is—just because Corelli tried to swindle him. Didn't succeed, just *tried*. Lublin did worse than that. He informed on Washburn. I guess Lublin has a right to be scared."

She was shaking her head. "It still doesn't add up," she said. "Last night, Lublin didn't know who the killers were. If he had known he would have told us, wouldn't he? I mean, assuming that he was telling us the truth. So how would he know who to call today? How would he know to set them after us?"

"That's easy."

She looked at him.

"All he had to do was ask Washburn," he said. "Jesus, I'm so stupid it's pathetic. He called Washburn and asked him who the men were, and Washburn told him without knowing what it was all about, and then he got in touch with them, with Lee and the other one. We went around playing detective, staking out his apartment, everything. All around Robin Hood's barn, for God's sake. We missed the shortcut."

"Where are you going?"

"To call Washburn."

He made the call from the telephone booth right there in the bar. At first he tried to find Washburn's number in the phone book, but there was no listing. Then he remembered and dug out his notebook. He had copied the number, along with the address, from Lublin's address book. He dropped a dime and dialed the number, and a soft-voiced woman picked up the phone almost immediately and said, "Mr. Washburn's residence."

He made his voice very New York. He asked if he could speak to Mr. Washburn, please. She wanted to know who was calling. Jerry Manna, he said. She asked if he would hold the line, please, and he said that he would.

Then a man's voice said, "Washburn here. Who's this?"

"Uh, I'm Jerry Manna, Mr. Washburn. I—"

"Who?"

"Jerry Manna, Mr. Washburn. Mr. Lublin said that I should call you. He said that—"

"Maurie?"

"Yes," Dave said. "I—"

"Hold it," Washburn said. He had a very deep voice and

137

spoke quickly, impatiently. "I don't like this phone. Give me your number, I'll get back to you. What's the number there?"

Could Washburn trace the call? He didn't think so. Quickly, he read off the telephone number. Washburn said, "Right, I'll get back to you," and broke the connection.

He sat in the phone booth, the door closed, and he wiped perspiration from his forehead. The palms of his hands were damp with sweat. Right now, he thought, Washburn could be calling Lublin. Lublin would tell him he never heard of a Jerry Manna. And then—

But why should Washburn be suspicious? Unless Lublin had told him everything after all. But Lublin wouldn't do that, because it didn't make any sense, that was the one thing Lublin had to avoid. And it took a long time to take a number and find out who it belonged to, where the phone was. The police could do it. Otherwise the phone company wouldn't give out the information. But Washburn was an important criminal, the kind who would have connections in the police department. One of them could get the information for him. Then he would stall on the phone, and a couple of goons would head for the bar.

They couldn't stay in the bar too long. If Washburn called back right away, they might be all right. But if he took too long it could be a trap.

Jill stood at the door of the phone booth, her eyebrows raised in question. He shook his head and waved her away. She went back to the table and poured beer into her glass, tilting the glass a few degrees and pouring the beer against the side of it. She raised the glass and sipped the beer.

The phone rang.

He reached for the receiver, fumbled it, knocked it off the hook. He grabbed it up and said, "Hello, Manna speaking."

Washburn said, "All right, I can talk now. What's the story?"

"Mr. Lublin said I should call you, Mr. Washburn."

"You said that already. What's it about?"

"It's about a builder from Hicksville," he said carefully. "A man named Joe. Maurie said—"

"What, again?"

He took a quick breath. *What, again?*

"You want to know the two boys on that, is that right?"

"That's right, Mr. Washburn. I—"

"Dammit, Maurie called me already today on that. When did you talk to him?"

"Last night."

"Well, he called here this morning. Early. He woke me up, dammit. I gave him all of that right then. Didn't you talk to him?"

"I can't reach him, Mr. Washburn. I tried him a couple of times. He maybe tried to get me, but I've been out and he couldn't call me where I've been. I thought I could take a chance and call you direct, Mr. Washburn, after I couldn't get hold of Maurie."

There was a long pause. Then Washburn said, "All right, dammit, but I hate these goddamned calls. They are two New York boys who work out of East New York near the Queens line. Lee Ruger is one, he's the one to talk to, and the other is Dago Krause. The price depends on the job, what they have to do. They get a good price because they do good work, they're reliable. That what you wanted?"

"If you could give me the address, Mr. Washburn, I would—"

"Yeah. Jesus, this is all stuff I told Maurie this morning. He got me out of bed for this, and now I've got to go over it all. This is a pain in the ass, you know that?"

"I really appreciate it, Mr. Washburn."

"Yeah. Just a minute." He waited, and Washburn came back and said, "I can't find the damned phone number. Krause's address I don't have, I never had it. Ruger's the one you want to talk to anyhow, see. That's 723 Lorring Avenue. There's a phone, you can probably find it. Maurie—"

"Thanks very much, Mr. Washburn."

Washburn wasn't through. "Maurie's a goddamned idiot," he said now. "He gave you my name, is that right?"

"Well, he—"

"He should damn well know better than that. What'd he do, just let it drop out?"

"More or less, Mr. Washburn."

"You tell him he should watch his mouth, you got that? Or I'll tell him myself. What did you say your name was? Manna?"

"Manna," he said. And, after Washburn rang off, he said, "From heaven."

# 13

THE ROYALTON was probably safe but they didn't go back there. Jill was afraid of the place, which was reason enough. Besides, it was vaguely possible that Ruger and Krause knew their names. The half hour after the murder of Corelli had been a time when everything happened too quickly, when everything was confused; even the memory of it was bright in some parts and hazy in others, and it was possible that the killers knew their names. They had registered under their right names at the Royalton, and if they ran a check from hotel to hotel—

But they had to get some rest. They walked half a block west on Thirty-fourth Street, and Dave went into a leather-goods store and bought a cheap suitcase. There was a haberdashery two doors down; he bought socks and underwear and two shirts there and packed them in the suitcase. Further down the same block they bought underwear and stockings for Jill.

They took a cab to a third-rate hotel on West Thirty-eighth between Eighth and Ninth, a place called the Moorehead. A sallow-faced clerk rented them a double room on the second floor, five-fifty a day, cash in advance. They registered as Mr. and Mrs. Ralph Cassiday of Albany, Georgia. There was an elevator but no operator to run it. The desk clerk took them upstairs and unlocked the door for them. He didn't wait for a tip.

The room held an old iron bedstead that had been repainted with white enamel long enough ago so that the paint had begun to flake away from the metal. The bed itself was a little smaller than a double, about three-quarter size. It sagged slightly in the middle. The bed linen was clean but old and worn. There was a dresser which had been repainted with brown enamel fairly recently. The painter had covered up the scars of neglected cigarettes without bothering to sand them down. Since then, three more burns had been added to the dresser top.

There was no rug. The floor was covered with brownish linoleum which was cracked in several places. The walls were a greenish gray, and very dirty. A fixture on the high ceiling held three unshaded light bulbs, one of which had burned out. A light cord hung down from the fixture over the center of the bed. The room had one window, which needed washing. It faced out upon a blank brick wall just a few feet away. The desk clerk had said that there was a bathroom down the hall.

He stood in the room, looking for some place to put the suitcase, finally setting it on top of the bed. She walked over to the window and opened it. "This is a dump," he said.

"It's all right."

"We could get out of here and go someplace better. Will you be able to sleep here? It's pretty bad."

"I don't mind. I think I could sleep anywhere, now."

He went over to her and put his arm around her. "Poor kid. You must be dead."

"Almost." She yawned. "This place isn't so bad. There's a bed—that's all I care about right now. What time is it?"

"Dinnertime."

"I'm not hungry. Are you?"

"No."

"We'll eat when we wake up. Right now I wouldn't know whether to order breakfast or dinner, anyway, so let's just get to sleep. We couldn't stay at a better hotel anyway, honey. We're such a mess they wouldn't take us in. Don't unpack the suitcase."

"Why not?"

"Because I wouldn't want to put any clothes in that dresser. None that I ever intended to wear. What are our names, incidentally? I didn't see what you wrote."

He told her.

"Cassiday," she said. "So many different names lately. Did you ever use phony names when you took other girls to motels?"

"Huh?"

"I bet you did. What names did you use?"

"Jesus," he said.

She grinned suddenly, a quick and wicked grin. Then she stepped away from him and began to unbutton her blouse. She took it off and asked him to unhook her bra. He did this. She took the bra off and crossed the room to set it and the blouse on the room's only chair, and he looked at her and was surprised when a sudden uncontrollable burst of desire shot through him. She began getting out of her skirt. He tried looking away from her but her body drew his eyes magnetically.

For God's sake, he thought. He turned away, toward the door, and said that he had to go downstairs for a minute.

"What for?"

"There's a drugstore on the corner," he said. "A few things I wanted to pick up."

"Just don't pick up any girls."

"Don't be silly."

She laughed happily at him. "First kiss me good-bye," she said.

He turned again. She was wearing a slip and stockings, nothing else. Her face was drawn with exhaustion and her skin was pale but this only served to make her still more desirable. She held her arms out to him and he caught her and kissed her. She pressed herself tightly against him and held the kiss.

When he let go of her she said, "I'll wait up for you."

"Don't."

"Well—"

"I might be a while," he said.

He wound up going to the drugstore after all. He bought a street guide there but it didn't do him much good. It told him what streets Lorring Avenue crossed, but he had never heard of any of those streets and wasn't even sure what borough East New York was in, or whether it was a separate suburb on Long Island. There was a West New York, he knew, and it was in New Jersey.

The drugstore had a pocket atlas of New York, with maps of the whole city, and he bought that. East New York turned out to be a part of Brooklyn. Brooklyn was a slightly lopsided diamond, and East New York was just above the eastern point of the diamond, north and west of Canarsie. He managed to find Lorring Avenue but couldn't figure out how to get there.

He bought two packs of cigarettes at the drugstore. He ate a candy bar. He weighed himself on a penny scale. According to the scale, he was a full twelve pounds under his normal weight, but he wasn't sure how accurate the scale might be.

He killed a few minutes that way to give Jill a chance to fall asleep. He could have made love to her, he thought. She would have let him, might even have been able to enjoy it, and God knew he wanted her, the passion no less strong because of its suddenness.

On the way back to the room he stopped at the floor's communal bathroom. He thought of taking a shower but changed his mind when he saw what the tub looked like. He washed his hands and face at the sink and went to the room, let himself in with his key. She was asleep, lying on top of the bedclothes, naked. She slept on her side facing the door with her knees bent, one arm under her head, the other up in front of her face. He saw the curves of her breasts.

He got undressed and lay down beside her, facing away from her. The bed was too small. Their bodies touched. She made a small sound in her sleep. He moved a little away from her and closed his eyes, trying to relax. He lay there for quite a while, wide awake, and then sleep came all at once.

# 14

<<<<<<<<<<<<<<<<<<<<<<<<<<<<<<<<<<<<<<<<<<<<<<<<<<<

THERE WAS this dream. In it, he was representing the plaintiff in a negligence action. His client had fallen down a department-store escalator and was suing for damages in the amount of sixty-five thousand dollars. The department-store floorwalker had just finished testifying that Dave's client had not fallen but had been pushed by a companion, as yet unidentified. Dave cross-examined. He argued brilliantly, but the defense witness ducked every question, slipping them off his shoulders and winking surreptitiously at Dave. There was no justice, he thought, frustrated, and he took out a gun and shoved the barrel into the man's slick face. He shouted questions at him and beat him over the head and shoulders with the butt of the gun. The man bled from the wounds and slumped in his chair. The judge pounded with his gavel, and Dave raised the gun and shot him. The bailiff moved toward him, gun drawn, and Dave shot him, too, and

turned toward the gallery and fired into the rows of spectators. The faces of the spectators melted away when his bullets hit them.

He woke up bathed in sweat. Jill was sitting on the edge of
the bed beside him, holding his shoulder and asking if
everything was all right. She was dressed and her face was
fresh and alive. The overhead light was on. He turned toward
the window. It was dark outside, still. He shook his head to
clear the dream away. She asked what was the matter.

"A dream," he said.

"A bad one?"

"An odd one. Very surrealistic."

"Dave—"

"It's nothing." He shook his head again and swung his
legs over the side of the bed. She was smoking a cigarette.
He took it from her and dragged on it. He asked her how
long she had been up.

"Just a few minutes."

"What time is it?"

"Four-thirty."

"The middle of the night," he said. He got dressed and
went down the hall to the bathroom to wash up. He had a
bad taste in his mouth and he needed a shave, but he hadn't
bought a razor or a toothbrush. He washed his mouth with
soap and gargled with tap water. He came back to the room,
put on a tie and knotted it carefully. "I look like hell," he
told her.

"You need a shave. That's all."

Outside, the streets were dark and empty. The corner
drugstore was closed. Even the bars were closed. He bought

a safety razor and a small pack of blades at an all-night drugstore on Forty-second Street. Down the block, Hector's cafeteria was open, one of four lighted spots on Times Square. The block itself was dark, movie marquees unlighted, almost every place closed. They got coffee and rolls at Hector's and he went upstairs to the men's room and shaved, lathering up with bar soap. He nicked himself, but not badly. When he was done he put the razor and the blades in a wastebasket and went back downstairs. His coffee had cooled off but he drank it anyway.

He said, "I was just thinking."

"About what?"

"Going back to Binghamton. It's going to feel funny, don't you think? Moving into the apartment, getting back to work."

"You mean after all of this?"

"Yes," he said. He got up and took their coffee cups back to the counter and had them filled again. He came back to the table and stirred his coffee methodically with a spoon. "Right back to another world," he said quietly. "Searching titles and filing deeds and drawing wills."

"That's not all you do."

"Well, no, but our kind of law is pretty quiet and orderly. You don't get up in the middle of the night. Or carry a gun."

She didn't say anything.

He sipped coffee and put the cup back on the saucer. "You'll be a housewife," he said.

"With a weekly bridge game, I suppose."

"Probably."

"Is it bad?"

"What—your bridge game? It's pretty bad."

She didn't smile. "That's not what I mean. Going back, and what our life will be like there."

"No, it's not bad. Why?"

"The way you were talking."

"I didn't mean it to sound that way," he said. "Just that it's very different from, well, this. What day is it?"

"I think Thursday."

"I'm supposed to pick up the Scranton papers. At that newsstand. I don't think I'll bother. Are you sure it isn't Friday?"

"No, it's Thursday."

"It seems longer. We haven't been married a week—can you believe that?"

"It does seem longer."

"I killed a man yesterday." He hadn't meant to say it. It had come out all by itself. *Nice day today. Maybe it'll rain. I killed a man yesterday. Want more coffee?*

"Don't think about it."

"I think I was dreaming about it. No one knows about it. You and I know, and Lublin knows, but no one else knows about it. Back home, nobody would dream it. If they heard about it they wouldn't believe it."

"So?"

"I was just thinking," he said.

They had to go back to the Moorehead. The gun was there, tucked between the mattress and the bedspring. The extra shells were in their room at the Royalton and he thought that a maid might stumble across them while she was cleaning the room. And the people at the Royalton might get sus-

picious if they didn't occupy the room at all. He decided
to call the hotel later in the day.

They locked the room door and went through the pocket
atlas to try to figure out the best way to get out to Lorring
Avenue. Two subways came close. There was an IND train
that ran out Pitkin Avenue, but he couldn't make out from
the maps how you picked up the train in the first place. It
seemed to originate somewhere in Brooklyn. One line of the
IRT Seventh Avenue ran as far as Livonia Avenue and Ashford Street, which would put them about a dozen short
blocks from Lorring. And he could figure out how to get that
train. They could take a cab, of course, but he wasn't sure
he could find a driver who would want to go all the way out
there, or who would know the route.

Downstairs, he left the key at the desk and paid another
five-fifty for the next night. They might return to the hotel
and they might not, but this way the room would be there
for them if they needed it in a hurry. The five-fifty was insurance.

They got on the subway at Thirty-fourth Street a few minutes before seven. The train was fairly empty at the start.
It thinned out even more at the Wall Street stop, and when
they crossed over into Brooklyn there were only five other
passengers in their car. He got up to check the map on the
wall of the car near the door. The train had a full twenty
stops to make in Brooklyn. A few people got on while the
train followed Flatbush Avenue; most of them left at the
Eastern Parkway stop. The .38 was in Dave's pants pocket
now. When he sat down his jacket came open, and he didn't
want the gun butt to show. The pocket that held the gun

bulged unnaturally and he kept fighting the impulse to pat it. No one seemed to notice the bulge.

The ride lasted forever. Once the train came up out of the earth and ran elevated for four stops before disappearing into the ground once more. Then it came up and stayed up. At a quarter after eight they hit the last stop, the end of the line. They were by then the only passengers in their car. They got off the train and walked to the staircase at the end of the subway platform. The sun was out but there was a strong breeze blowing that chilled the air. They went down the stairs and passed through a turnstile.

He found a street sign. They were at the corner of New Lots and Livonia. He dug out the pocket atlas and thumbed to the map of that area, trying to figure out which direction to take next. He knew what route they had to take but he couldn't tell which way they were facing or how to start off. He looked back at the subway platform, trying to orient himself, and Jill nudged him. He looked up and saw a uniformed policeman heading across the intersection toward them. The only thing he could think of was the gun. The cop knew about it, the cop was coming to pick him up. He was almost ready to start running when he realized he was acting crazy. The cop came closer and asked if they were lost, if he could help.

Dave laughed now, unable to help it. The cop looked at him curiously. He broke off the laughter and said yes, they were lost, and asked how to get to Lorring Avenue. The cop gave him directions—two blocks over Ashford to Linden Boulevard, then a dozen or so blocks to the left on Linden and he couldn't miss it. They thanked the cop and left.

The neighborhood was a marginal slum, less densely pop-

ulated than a Manhattan slum would be, but run-down and
dirty, with a similar air of chronic depression. Most of the
houses were only two or three stories tall. They were set close
together with no driveways and no lawns. Stores were beginning to open, kids walked to school in bunches. About a
third of the kids were Negroes.

Further along Linden Boulevard the neighborhood im-
proved a little. The housing there was similar to where
Corelli had lived in Hicksville, two-story semidetached brick
fronts. The lawns here were smaller, and few of them had
more than scattered patches of weeds springing up from
hard-packed dirt. There were trees, but they were scrawny.

"I made a mistake," he told her. They were waiting for a
light to change. "I told that cop Lorring Avenue. He could
remember."

She didn't answer him. He lit a fresh cigarette, thinking
that this was something new, another unfamiliar element.
The policeman was to be feared, to be avoided. He should
have just asked the way to Linden Boulevard and found his
own way from there. There were so many things to learn, a
whole new approach to social phenomena that had to be
fixed in the mind.

At Fountain Avenue, Linden Boulevard cut forty-five degrees to the left. Lorring Avenue started across the intersection from it, running due east. It was almost entirely residential. Here and there an older building remained, with a
grocery store or delicatessen on the ground floor and apartments over it. The rest of the homes were semidetached
brick fronts, blocks of them, all very much the same. Most
of the houses had very tall television antennas. The cars at

curbs or in driveways were Fords and Plymouths and Ramblers and Chevys. There were a lot of station wagons and a few Volkswagens.

When they crossed Grant Street, they moved into an older part of the neighborhood and the scenery changed abruptly. For half a block there were brick fronts on one side of Lorring, but the rest of that block and the other side of the street were made up of older frame houses, larger buildings set somewhat further back from the street. A sign in the front window of one white-clapboard house announced that tourists were welcome.

The block after Grant was Elderts Lane. Lee Ruger lived at 723 Lorring, between Elderst and Forbell. His house, like several others on that block, was three stories tall. A wooden sign on the lawn said "Rooms," and a small metal strip on the front of the house beside the door said "Rooms for Rent."

They walked past the house and kept walking almost to the end of the block. The Pontiac they had seen yesterday was not at the curb, nor had they seen it alongside the house. It might be at the back, in the rear of the driveway or in a garage.

He said, "I don't know if he's home or not. I didn't see the car. Of course, it might be Krause's car, the one we saw."

"They don't live together?"

"I don't think so. They might share an apartment, but this is just a furnished room. They wouldn't share a room. Unless they both have rooms in the same building. There's still a lot we don't know. We have to know whether or not anybody's home." The gun was still in his pocket, and its weight made him uncomfortable. He looked around quickly to make sure no one was watching him, then took the gun from the pocket and jammed it once again beneath the waistband of his slacks.

"This is crazy," he said.

"What is?"

"What we're doing now. Standing on the corner waiting for him to come by in a car and blow our brains out. I feel like a target, standing here in the open."

"We could call up and—"

"The hell with it," he said. "I don't want to call him. A phone call would only put him on guard if he is home, anyway. And I'm sick of calling people on the phone. Look, there are two possibilities. He's there or he isn't. If he isn't home, I want to know about it, and I also want to get upstairs and search his room. Or take another room at the house so that we can sandbag him when he comes in."

"What's sandbag?"

"Surprise him, I don't know. They say it on television. If he *is* home, there's no sense waiting in the shadows for him to leave the house. He might be there now, lying in bed, sound asleep. It's still early. He could be sleeping. If he's home, the only thing to do is go upstairs and kill him."

She shivered.

"That's what we came for," he said.

"I know. Would you shoot him in bed?"

"If I got the chance." Her eyes were lowered. He cupped her chin with his right hand and raised her face so that her eyes met his. "Listen to me," he said. "It's not fair play. Fine. We are not playing. They were not playing before, not with Corelli and not with us, and we are not playing now. I'm not Hopalong Cassidy. I don't want to be a good sport and let that bastard draw against me. I'd much rather shoot him in the back, or while he's sleeping."

He watched as she put her tongue out to lick her lower lip. "All right," she said.

"Do you understand, Jill?"

"I understand."

"Are you sure?"

"Yes. Only—"

"Only what?"

"Nothing," she said. He waited, and she started to say something else, then gripped his arm and pointed. He spun around. A car was coming toward them down Lorring, a car the color of the one they had seen at Gramercy Park the day before. He shoved Jill behind him and dropped automatically to one knee. His hand went for the gun. The front sight snagged momentarily on his clothing. Then he got the gun out. The car came closer.

It was a convertible, though, and it wasn't a Pontiac; it was a Dodge, and a woman was driving it. There were two kids and three bags of groceries in the back seat. The car passed them, and he looked at the gun in his hand and felt like an idiot. He shoved it under his waistband and got to his feet. She said, "I thought—"

"So did I." He pointed down Forbell Avenue. There were stores a block away at the corner. "Go down there," he said.

"Why?"

"Because you'd be in the way now. I have to go inside, and I have to go alone."

"Now?"

"Now. There's no sense waiting. That car wasn't them, but

the next one might be, and we're perfect targets like this. Go on."

She hesitated, then turned and went. He waited until she was a few doors down the block. Then he went back to 723 and walked quickly to the front door. A sticker on the windowpane said "We Gave." There was a red feather under the inscription. There were curtains behind the window and he couldn't see into the house. He tried the door. It was locked. He rang the bell.

Nothing happened. He took a breath and rang the bell again. An angry voice, sounding neither male nor female, said, "I'm coming!" He waited. There were footsteps, coming closer, and he put his hand inside his jacket and let his fingers settle on the butt of the .38. The metal felt very warm now.

The door opened warily. He saw a face, and for a shadow of a second he thought it was Lee's face and he tensed his hand to draw the gun. Then the door opened wider, and he saw that it was a woman, an old woman with rheumy eyes and a mannish moustache. Her hair was black, sprinkled with flat gray. She looked at him and waited for him to say something.

"Does Lee Ruger live here?"

"Ruger?" She looked at him. "He's here," she said. "Why?"

"Is he home?"

She looked exasperated. "Eight rooms here," she said. She drew the door open, stepped back. "Eight rooms, and seven of 'em rented. You think I own this place? I just run it, I get the rent, I make sure it's clean. You expect me to keep track of who's here and who isn't? I got enough without that."

He entered the house, looked over her shoulder at the staircase. There was a table at the second-floor landing. On it was a vase of withered flowers. The house smelled of cigarette smoke and old furniture. He said, "Ruger—"

"Room Six. If he's here he's in it. If he's not he's not. You want to go upstairs, then go. The top floor."

She didn't wait to be thanked. She turned bulkily and went back to the kitchen and he started up the stairs. They creaked under his feet. At first he tried to walk softly and slowly, placing his feet on the edges of the steps to cut down their creaking. But it didn't matter whether or not anyone heard his approach. Now he was just another man walking up the flight of stairs.

The dying flowers at the second-floor landing were roses, their petals mostly gone. He thought, The woman can be a witness, she can identify me. But that didn't matter either, he decided. Her description would not be enough to lead the police to him, and if he were picked up by them, they wouldn't need her as a witness. If he and Jill were picked up, they would confess. He was fairly sure of this.

He climbed another flight of stairs to the top floor. There were four rooms on the floor, four doors off the small hallway. Room 6 was at the end of the hall away from the staircase. The door was closed. He walked over to the door and tried to listen for movement inside the room. He couldn't hear anything. Downstairs, in another part of the rooming house, someone flushed a toilet. The noise carried clearly. He waited while the plumbing noises died down and listened again at the door. No sounds came from within.

He took the gun out and held it in his right hand. He positioned himself at the side of the door and held the gun so that it was pointed just above and slightly to the side of the knob. His finger curled expectantly around the trigger. He held his breath for a moment, then let it out slowly, then breathed in again. With his left hand he reached for the doorknob.

# 15

<<<<<<<<<<<<<<<<<<<<<<<<<<<<<<<<<<<<<<<<<<<<<<<<<<

THE ROOM was anticlimactically empty. The door was not locked. He turned the knob and threw the door open, gun in hand, like Broderick Crawford bulling his way into George Raft's hideout, and the room was empty. He stood in the doorway looking at an unmade empty bed. Cigar butts filled an ashtray on the bedside table. There were ashes on the floor. He stepped inside and pulled the door shut quickly. He started to bolt the door, then decided that was crazy. He took a deep breath and sat down on the edge of the unmade bed and put the gun down beside him, then remembered and rotated the gun's cylinder so that there was no bullet under the chamber.

Ruger wasn't around. But this was Ruger's room and the man would come back to it, sooner or later. And he would be waiting for him. Ruger would open the door and he, Dave, would be sitting on Ruger's bed with a gun in his hand, waiting.

The bathroom. He remembered the flushing of the toilet and thought that Ruger might still be in the house. He could be in the bathroom on a lower floor. He could bump into the woman and find out that a man had come to his room, looking for him.

He ran his hand over the bed linen. It was cool, and he guessed that it hadn't been slept in for hours. He picked up the ashtray and several of the cigar butts. They were cold and smelled stale. The air in the room was also stale, and there was a thin layer of dust over the chair and dresser and night table. It didn't look as though anyone had been in the room in a day or more. Just to make sure, he slipped out of the room and walked halfway down the stairs. The door of the second-floor bathroom was slightly ajar. He perched himself on the stairs and waited until the bathroom's occupant finished and left. It was a man, a very old man who walked with a slight limp, carrying a towel and a toothbrush and an old-fashioned straight razor down the hall to his room.

So Ruger was out. He got to his feet and went back up to the third floor again and let himself into Ruger's room once more. He closed the door and walked over to the window. There were curtains, lacy ones that didn't quite fit the image of the hired killer. He pushed them apart and looked out through the window. It needed washing, and the room needed airing out. He opened the window three inches at top and bottom and looked out through the glass. A small boy was riding his bicycle in the street, poised precariously on a seat that was too high for him. The boy rode off. A sports car breezed by and cornered sharply at Elderts Lane. A mailman, his leather sack bulging, walked down one driveway and up another.

Perfect, he thought. Ruger was out, and sooner or later Ruger would come back. Alone, or with Dago Krause in tow. Either way, he would be able to see them coming from the window. That was luck, the window facing the street. Ruger couldn't get to the house without being seen on the way. He would be ready for him, ready and waiting.

His mind hurried ahead, sketching in the details. The escape shouldn't be too difficult. There would be no gun battle to draw attention, because Ruger wouldn't know he was there until it was too late for him to do anything about it. There would only be one shot, the one he himself would fire. People would hear it, but few people ever recognized a single shot for what it was. A truck backfiring, a kid with a firecracker—no one ever thought it was a gunshot. And by the time people reacted to the shot he would be on his way out of the house.

Jill, thank God, was out of the way around the corner. He would kill Ruger and get clear of the house. He would hurry around the corner and find her, and then they would grab a cab back to Manhattan or get onto a subway, anything at all. All he had to do was wait.

Fingerprints. With Ruger's body left behind, the police would be all over the place checking for prints. And his were on file. He had been printed in the army, and he had vague memories of his fingerprints having been taken years ago as a matter of course when he held a summer job with the Broome County welfare department. He went around the room wiping the things he had touched—the doorknob, the ashtray, the window. He did a thorough job, then hauled Ruger's chair over to the window and cleared a pile of dirty clothes off the seat. He sat down facing the window and waited.

Time crawled. Three cigarettes later he got up from the chair and began searching Ruger's room. There might be something the police shouldn't find, he thought. A note mentioning Washburn or Lublin or Corelli, anything that would enable the cops to make a connection between Ruger and them. But there was nothing like that. Ruger's room was strangely barren of artifacts of any sort. There were two or three paperbound books, their bindings cracked and pages dog-eared. There was a mimeographed thirty-page pamphlet of hard-core pornography illustrated with crude drawings and featuring a sadomasochistic theme and a semiliterate prose style. There were clothes, selected with little evident thought for quality or fashion. There were no guns, so Ruger was evidently carrying one—Dave couldn't believe the man could get along without owning one. There was a knife, a switchblade stiletto with a five-inch blade. The edge was quite sharp. There was a homemade blackjack—a length of lead pipe with a leather loop for a handle and several thicknesses of black electrical tape wrapped around the pipe.

No notes, no addresses, no telephone numbers. There was a key, evidently to a safe-deposit box somewhere. Dave pocketed it; there was no telling what the police might find in the box, and he decided it couldn't hurt to keep them from it.

He wiped everything clean of prints and sat down again.

Outside, the street was calm and clear. He wondered how long it would be before Ruger came back. If the man had been out hunting them all night long, he would probably be tired, ready to sleep. But he might have slept. He could have spent the night with a girl, or anywhere.

And his mind filled suddenly with a picture of Ruger with a girl and then of Ruger with Jill. He closed his eyes and gritted his teeth painfully. The image passed and he opened his eyes again and gazed again out the window.

How long? It was going slowly enough for him, there in Ruger's room, and he realized how much more slowly it must be going for Jill. She didn't know what was happening, where he was, where Ruger was—she was stuck around the corner and had no idea what was happening or when she would see him again. He pictured her sitting over a cup of coffee and not knowing for certain whether he was alive or dead, and he realized all at once what a bad arrangement this was.

She should have stayed in the hotel, of course. He had suggested that, briefly, but as he said it he had known she wouldn't go along with it. And once he decided to go straight up after Ruger, he should have sent her back to the city to wait for him. She probably would have put up an argument but he might have been able to talk her into it.

This way, everything was up in the air. She was close by but not close enough to know what was going on. He thought of leaving the rooming house for a minute. He could duck around the corner, find her, let her know what was happening, and then get her into a cab headed for their hotel. But if he left the room, how could he get back in? He might not be able to bluff his way past the woman again. Even if he managed that, it would just get her wondering, and if she wondered enough she might make a point of tipping Ruger off when he came through the door.

And if he left the place, Ruger could come back while he was looking for Jill. He wouldn't know about it one way or the other and he could come bouncing up the stairs into a trap he wouldn't be able to get out of. As things stood, he had the advantage, he held all the cards. But if he left the room he would be chancing the loss of that edge. He couldn't risk it.

She would just have to wait.

He reached for a cigarette. There were only two left in his pack, and he didn't have a spare. He hesitated, then shrugged and took out one of the cigarettes and lit it.

They drove up just as he was finishing the cigarette. He saw the car coming down Lorring, moving slowly toward the house, and he dropped his cigarette to the floor and covered it with his foot. He took hold of the gun, spun the cylinder to put a bullet under the hammer once again. It was their car this time. The Pontiac, and the right color, and coasting to a stop in front of the house and across the street.

He opened the window a little wider at the bottom and drew the curtains almost shut. Looking down, he could see them through the front windshield. Ruger was on the passenger side and Krause was behind the wheel. They were sitting there now, making no move to leave the car.

Come on, he thought. Both of you. Come on.

He rested the gun barrel on the windowsill. They were still in the car. They might both drive away, he thought. They might change their minds and drive away and leave him there. His grip tightened on the butt of the gun, and beads of sweat dotted his forehead. He couldn't breathe.

A car door opened, on Ruger's side. One of them spoke in an undertone. They both laughed. Then Ruger was coming and Krause was driving off, he thought. He was both glad and sorry. He wanted them both, right away, but one would be better than none at all.

*Hurry up, dammit—*

Ruger put a foot out of the car, then drew it back in again. Dave gritted his teeth. Ruger swung the foot out again, then shifted his weight and stepped out of the Pontiac. He stood with one hand on the open door and the other on the roof of the car. He was talking with Krause but Dave couldn't hear anything.

He straightened up, then, and slammed the car door shut. Krause gunned the motor. Ruger nodded to him, and Krause pulled off, slowed down briefly for the stop sign at Forbell and continued east on Lorring. Ruger stood watching the Pontiac until it disappeared from view. He made no move to cross the street.

Dave aimed the gun at him, tentatively. He lowered it and looked at the man. For the first time, he didn't know if he could do it. He did not know if he could shoot him.

His words to Jill: "Listen to me. It's not fair play. Fine. We are not playing." But it was less clear-cut when you had time to think about it, less certain when you had the man centered in your sights.

He watched Ruger. The gunman seemed stubbornly determined to wait forever before he crossed the street. He reached into his breast pocket now and drew out a stubby cigar. Dave watched as he unwrapped the cigar slowly, carefully. He dropped the cellophane wrapper. It fell to the sidewalk and the wind played with it. Ruger bit off the end of the cigar, spat it out, took out a windproof lighter, thumbed it open, lit the cigar, closed the lighter, returned it to his pocket, and puffed on the cigar. He moved to the curb and glanced across the street.

Then Dave saw him glance to his right, saw the cigar drop unnoticed to the street. Ruger was staring. Dave grabbed the curtains, tugged them aside.

*Jill.*

She had just turned the corner. She was walking toward the rooming house, looking straight ahead. He looked at Ruger. The man had a gun in his hand, he recognized her.

He yelled, "Jill, get back!"

He saw Jill look up, then clap one hand to her mouth. Ruger shot at her, missed, spun around to look up at the window. Dave pointed the .38 and squeezed the trigger. The sound was deafening and the recoil jolted up his arm to his shoulder. Jill had not moved. He yelled at her to get back, to get the hell out of the way. She hesitated and then spun abruptly around and dashed for the corner. Ruger looked at her but did not shoot. He aimed the gun at the third-story window, steadied himself, and fired.

# 16

<<<<<<<<<<<<<<<<<<<<<<<<<<<<<<<<<<<<<<<<<<<<<<<<<<<<

RUGER'S SHOT went off to the left. It slammed into the house a few feet to the side of the window and the whole house seemed to rock. Dave kicked the chair back out of his way and dropped into a crouch in front of the window. He looked out. Ruger was crouching, too, trying to present the smallest possible target. He looked around for a place to hide himself but stayed where he was. The trees there were young ones, too small to hide behind, and the nearest parked cars were three doors down the street.

Dave shot at him. This time his arm anticipated the recoil and the gun stayed steady. He missed; the bullet dug into the pavement a few feet in front of Ruger. Ruger snapped off a shot in reply. It shattered the window and glass flew.

Down the street a car stopped with a screech of brakes,

spun in a ragged U-turn that took it a few feet over the curb, and sped off in the opposite direction. Somewhere a woman screamed. Ruger ran halfway across the lawn behind him, stopped, crouched, fired. His shot wasn't even close.

Ruger was up again, running in a crouch, zigzagging toward the side of the house behind him. Dave followed him with the gun, his elbows braced on the windowsill, holding the .38 with both hands now. Ruger stopped, and as he started to spin once more around he was no longer a moving target. Dave gave the trigger a gentle squeeze.

He had not really believed the shot would be on target. But the bullet tore into Ruger's arm above the elbow and sent his gun flying. The impact of the shot spun Ruger halfway around and knocked him to the ground. He moved awkwardly there, using his good arm to push himself to his feet. The bad arm hung like deadweight.

He got up and turned toward Dave, then away from him. His arm was leaking blood. He had lost his bearings and looked this way and that like a nearsighted man searching for his eyeglasses.

Dave aimed again and fired again, and the bullet took Ruger in the small of the back. He shrieked like a girl and went down flat on his face and didn't move.

Now the whole house was awake. Dave yanked the door open, tore out of the room. A woman across the hallway was looking at him from her door. He glanced at her and she drew back in terror, slamming the door shut after her. He raced down the stairs. At the second floor, a burly man in his undershirt stepped into his path. Dave hit him across the face with the barrel of the gun, shoved him and sent him flying.

On the ground floor, a woman was shouting. There was nobody in sight. The front door was wide open. He ran through it, down the steps, along the path to the street. Across the street Ruger lay bleeding. Dave ran over to him. Ruger lay on his face, his body twitching spasmodically, a low moan issuing from his lips. Dave knelt momentarily and put the muzzle of the gun to the back of Lee Ruger's head. He barely heard the roar of the gun as his last bullet tore into Ruger's brain.

The neighborhood screamed with excitement. Doors slammed, windows opened. A police siren sounded in the distance. He was running now, not thinking, just running at top speed. His heart pounded violently and there was a constant roaring in his ears, like wind in a tunnel. He turned at the corner and kept running. Jill was up ahead, staring openmouthed at him. He ran to her.

"Dave, I didn't know. Are you all right? Are you all right?"

He couldn't answer her. He turned her around and grabbed her arm and they ran.

# 17

<<<<<<<<<<<<<<<<<<<<<<<<<<<<<<<<<<<<<<<<<<<<<<<<<<<<

IN THE CAB he moved the gun from one pocket to the other.
He could smell powder burns on his hands and it seemed
to him that the whole back seat of the taxi reeked of the
smell, that the driver couldn't help noticing it. He sat stiffly
in his seat, trying not to look over his shoulder for policemen.
They had caught the cab on Linden Boulevard, and they
were already approaching the Manhattan Bridge, so they
seemed to be in the clear, but he couldn't shake off the feeling that carloads of police were hot on their trail.

They crossed over into Manhattan. He waited for guilt to
claim him, waited to be moved once again by a feeling of
having crossed a great moral boundary. But this did not happen. He felt that he had been a very lucky bungler. He had
very nearly gotten Jill killed, and had watched a prospec-

tive one-sided ambush turn into a gun battle. Good shooting and good position had won the battle, and pure blind luck had let them get out uncaught from the mess he had created. He was ashamed of the bungling and grateful for the luck. But the confused guilt that had come over him after he had killed the bodyguard in Lublin's house—this did not come now. He wondered why.

They got out of the cab at Forty-second Street and ducked into a cafeteria. He went to the counter to get coffee and stood in line just long enough to decide that he didn't want coffee. He left the line and took Jill around the corner. There was a bar there, and it was open already. They sat at a table. He had a straight shot of bar rye with a beer chaser. She didn't want anything.

They lit cigarettes, and she said, "I'm so stupid, I almost ruined everything. I thought I was being so good at all this. And then like an idiot—"

"What happened?"

"I don't know. I kept waiting and waiting and you didn't come. I didn't know what was happening. I couldn't stand it."

"It's all right now."

"I know." She closed her eyes for a moment, then opened them. "I'm okay. It was the waiting. I thought I was very brave. When I went to Lublin's—"

"You were a little too brave then."

"But it was easy. I was doing something, I could see what was going on. This time all I could do was stand around and find things to worry about. I had to see what was going on. I picked a hell of a time, didn't I?"

"It was a bad arrangement. Forget it."

"I'm sorry."

"Don't be sorry. We're out of it."

"Are you sure he's—"

"Yes, he's dead." The *coup de grâce*, the bullet in the back of the skull. Yes, Lee was dead.

"Did anyone see you?"

"Half the world saw me."

"Will they find us?"

"I don't think so." He sipped beer. "They'll know what we look like, but they won't know where to look for us, or who to look for. The big worry was that we might have been picked up on the spot. They would have had us then, and cold. A dozen different people could have identified me. But I think we're out of it now."

"What now?"

"Now we check out of the Royalton," he said. "I was going to call them and tell them to hold our room. But that's silly. If we're not going to stay there, we might as well clear out altogether. And there are things there that we need."

"What?"

"Our clothes and all. And the rest of the bullets."

"I forgot that."

"For Krause," he said.

There was no problem at the Royalton. They went to their room and packed, and he called the desk and told them to make out the bill and to get the car ready. He packed everything and took the suitcases downstairs himself. The hotel took his check. The doorman brought the Ford around, and Dave gave him a dollar and loaded the suitcases into the back seat. They got into the car. He drove around until he found a Kinney garage on Thirty-sixth Street between Eighth and Ninth and left the car there. They carried the suitcases back to the Moorehead and walked upstairs to their room there instead of waiting for the ancient elevator.

Around four in the afternoon he went around the corner and came back with a deck of cards, a six-pack of ginger ale and a bottle of V.O. They played a few hands of gin rummy and drank their drinks out of water tumblers. There was no ice. At six he found a delicatessen and brought back sandwiches. They ate in the room and drank more of the ginger ale, plain this time. He brought back a paper, but they couldn't find anything about Ruger.

"You never did get those Scranton papers," she said.

"So we're out a dollar."

Later he felt like talking about the shooting. He told her how he had sat at the window watching Ruger with the cigar, how he had pointed the gun at him, how he had felt.

"I don't think I could have shot him just like that," he said.

"But you did."

"Because all hell broke loose. There was no time to debate the morality of it, not with the bastard shooting at us."

"You would have killed him anyway."

"I don't know. I don't feel bad about it. Not even uneasy."

"How do you feel?"

"I don't know."

"I feel relieved," she said.

"Relieved?"

"That we're both alive. And that he's not, too. We came here to do something, and we've done part of it, and we're still safe and all right, and I feel relieved about that."

They went to sleep early. They had both gotten a little

drunk. She didn't get sick, just sleepy. They got undressed and into bed, and the liquor made sleep come easily. And there was no attempt at lovemaking to complicate things, not this time. He held her and kissed her and they were close, and then he rolled aside and they slept.

In the morning she asked what they were going to do now, about Dago Krause.

"Lie low for a little while," he said.

"Here at the hotel?"

"It's as good a place as any. If we let things cool down, we'll be in a better position. There's the cops to think about, for one thing. With Ruger's murder so fresh, they'll be on their toes. If they have a little time to relax they'll just let it ride in the books as another gang killing. They won't break their necks looking for us or keeping a watch on Krause. You remember the amount of attention they paid to Corelli's death. Everybody was delighted to find an excuse not to try finding Corelli's murderers. It'll be the same here. They'll decide Ruger was killed by a professional, and they'll bury the whole thing in the files.

"The same thing with Krause, in another way. He'll be on guard right now. He won't tell the police anything. He'll be sure we're coming for him, and he'll walk around with eyes in the back of his head. In three days he'll manage to con-vince himself that one killing was enough to satisfy us or that we panicked once Ruger was dead and beat it out of the city. Let him relax."

"How will we find him?"

"We'll find him."

"He won't be in the phone book. I mean, there must be a million Krauses, even if he has a phone, and we don't know

177

his first name. Just a nickname. Why do you suppose they call him Dago? Krause isn't an Italian name, is it?"

"No. We'll find him."

"How?"

"We'll find him. One way or another, we'll find him."

They spent the morning in the hotel room. At noon he went to the drugstore and picked up a stack of magazines, plus the morning papers. All the papers had the story, but not even the tabloids gave it a very big play. It wasn't good copy. There had been a gun battle of sorts, which was on the plus side, but no innocent bystanders had been killed, and since no one had spotted Jill there was no sex angle to work on. The prevailing theory seemed to be that Ruger had been killed by a professional killer, a common enough ending for a criminal. The eyewitness reports contradicted one another incredibly, and the composite description of the killer made him about thirty-five, shorter and heavier than Dave. The whole pattern of the killing itself was confused in the papers. One witness insisted that Ruger had been ambushed by two men, one firing from the rooming house and the other gunning him down from behind a parked car. The woman at Ruger's place told reporters that the killer had showed her false credentials and had posed as a federal officer.

They read all the articles together, and he laughed and folded up the papers and carried them down the hall and stuffed them in a large wastebasket. "I thought so," he told Jill. "They would have had to pick us up on the spot in order to get us. Now they're a million miles away."

They went out for lunch and sat a long time with coffee and cigarettes. They walked up to Forty-second Street. There were a pair of science-fiction movies playing at the Victory, and the daytime rates were less than a dollar. It seemed like too much of a bargain to pass up. They walked in somewhere around the middle of a British import about a lost colony on Alpha Centauri and sat in the balcony. The theater was fairly crowded. They watched the end of that picture, a newsreel, three cartoons, a slew of coming attractions, and the other movie, one in which the fate of the world is menaced by giant lemmings, beasts that rushed pell-mell to the sea and devoured all the human beings in their path. Then there were more trailers, and they saw the Alpha Centauri movie up to the point where they had come in.

There was a comfortable feeling of security in the theater, a feeling of being in a crowd but not of it, of being surrounded by other persons while remaining comfortably anonymous. At first they were tense and on guard, but this stopped, and they got quickly lost in the action on the screen.

He picked up the evening papers on the way back to the hotel. In the room, he checked through them while Jill went down the hall to wash out underwear and stockings in the bathroom sink. He didn't expect to find anything much in the papers, just checked them out methodically as a matter of form. For the most part, the material on the shooting was just a rehash of the stories in the morning papers, with a little extra material on Ruger's background and criminal record and some hints at the police investigation of the murder.

But a final paragraph in one article said:

> Philip "Dago" Krause, described by police as a longtime friend and associate of the murdered man, was among those brought in for questioning. Krause, who lives at 2792 23rd Avenue in Astoria, has a record of arrests dating back to 1948. He was released after close interrogation. . . .

He took the paper down the hall to Jill and showed it to her. "Look at that," he said, excited. "I told you we'd find him. The damned fools drew us a map."

That night they had dinner at a good steak house on West Thirty-sixth Street. They went back to the hotel and drank more V.O. The ginger ale was gone. He drank his straight, and she mixed hers with tap water. They played gin rummy part of the time and spent the rest of the time sitting around reading magazines. She washed out some socks for him and hung them on the curtain rod over the window to dry. She muttered something about playing housewife on her honeymoon, and he smiled thoughtfully. It was the first time in days that either of them had mentioned the word "honeymoon."

The next day was Saturday. There was nothing new on Ruger's killing in any of the papers. Most of them had dropped it. One of the tabloids had a brief and pointless follow-up piece, but that was about all there was. They stayed close to the hotel.

By Sunday she was getting impatient, anxious to get it over and done with. "It's better to wait," he said. "Another couple of days. It won't be long now." They spent the afternoon at another Forty-second Street movie house and had dinner at the Blue Ribbon, on Forty-fourth Street. They had drinks before dinner and steins of Wurzburger with their meal and brandy with the coffee, and they were feeling the drinks by the time they left the place. He wanted to go back to the Moorehead, but she suggested stopping at a jazz place down the street and he went along with it. They sat at a circular bar and listened to a man play piano, until she lowered her head suddenly and fastened her fingers around his wrist.

She said, "Don't look up. Not now."

"What's the matter?"

"There's a man across the bar, he was one of the ones at Lublin's that night. I don't remember his name but I met him there. The one with the red tie. Don't look straight at him, but see if he's looking at us."

He saw the man she meant, watched him out of the corner of his eye. The man hadn't seemed to notice them yet.

"He may not recognize me," she said softly. "I looked different then, and I think he was drunk that night, anyway. Is he looking this way?"

"No."

"We'd better get out of here. Let me go first." She slipped off her stool. He left change on the bar and followed her out the door. Outside, she stood leaning against the side of the building and breathing heavily. He took her arm and led her down the street. A cab stopped for them. They got in and rode back to the hotel without saying a word.

In the room she said, "It's dangerous. The more time we spend in this city—"

"I know." He lit a cigarette. "Tomorrow."

"Is that too soon?"

"No. I was going to wait until Tuesday or Wednesday, but you're right, we can't stick around here too long. It was only a matter of time before we bumped into somebody. It was lucky he didn't spot us."

"Yes."

"And lucky you recognized him."

He stayed with her until after midnight. Then he left the hotel and walked downtown for a dozen blocks. On a dark side street he found a two-year-old Chevy with New Jersey license plates. The plates were in frames fastened by bolts. He used a quarter to loosen the bolts, took both plates, and carried them back to the hotel inside his shirt.

They packed up everything except the gun and the box of shells. He loaded the revolver with five bullets and carried the remaining shells outside to another dark street. There were about fifteen shells left in the box. He dropped them one by one into a sewer and chucked the empty carton into a mailbox.

At seven the next morning, he left the hotel again and walked to the Kinney garage. The place was just opening. He got his car, paid the attendant three and a half dollars, and parked the car on the street a few doors down from the hotel. He went upstairs for the luggage. Jill came down with him. She had the gun in her purse. They walked down to where the car was parked and loaded their bags into the trunk and locked it. He drove the car and she sat close beside him. He took the West Side Drive uptown to Ninety-fifth Street, then drove around the side streets between Broadway and West End Avenue until he found what he was looking for, an alleyway alongside a warehouse. He drove through the alley to the back of the warehouse and switched license plates, bolting the New Jersey plates loosely to the car and putting his own plates in the trunk of the Ford. He backed out of the alley and drove up to 125th Street and swung east to the Triborough Bridge.

They crossed the bridge. The heavy traffic was coming

across the bridge into Manhattan, rush-hour commuters coming into the city. He drove through Astoria, and she checked the route in the pocket atlas and told him which turns to take. They made only one wrong turn; it took them three blocks out of their way, but they found their mistake and got back where they belonged. He found Krause's block and then Krause's building and drove around looking for a parking place. The only spot was next to a fire hydrant. He drove around the block twice, and by the second time around someone had come out and moved a car. It was a tight fit, but he managed to squeeze the Ford into the space.

He killed the motor, got out of the car. He walked around to the curb side while she moved over behind the wheel. He got in and sat beside her. Her purse, with the .38 in it, was on the seat between them. From where he sat he had a good view of the entrance to Krause's apartment building. It was about half a block away, on their side of the street.

And Krause was home. Dave could see the gunmetal Pontiac just across the street from Krause's building. Krause was inside, and he would not stay there forever.

"This time," he said quietly, "we do it right."

She nodded. Her hands gripped the steering wheel securely and her eyes were fixed straight ahead. He offered her a cigarette but she didn't want one.

His window was up. He rolled it all the way down.

He said, "The easy way, the simple way. Listen, back up as far as you can, and swing the wheel so that we can get out of here in a hurry. We don't want to be stuck in this spot."

She did as he told her, backing the car all the way against the car behind them and turning the wheel so that they would be able to pull out quickly when the time came. He smoked his cigarette and flicked the ashes out of the open window.

Waiting, he thought, was always the hardest part. Once things began to happen, a good percentage of your actions were automatic. You didn't have to sit and think, and you had no time to worry, no chance to second-guess yourself. But waiting required a special sort of personal discipline. You had to accept that stretch of time as something to be endured, a wasted period during which you turned yourself off and let the time pass by itself.

His mind went over details. He tested the plan from every angle, and each time it held up. It was simple and direct. There were no little tangles to it, no sharp corners that could catch and snag. It held.

And they waited.

A few people left Krause's building. Two or three entered it. One time he saw a man framed in the doorway who looked very much like Krause, and he had to look a second time before he realized it was someone else. He felt annoyingly conspicuous, sitting like this in a parked car, but he told himself that it was safe enough. No one would pay any attention to them. People sat in parked cars. There was no law against it. And the people who walked past them seemed in too much of a hurry to waste valuable time noticing them.

It was cool out, and once he started to roll up the window. She asked what he was doing, and he caught himself and rolled the window down again. He reached over and opened her purse. The gun was there, waiting.

At twenty-five minutes after ten, Dago Krause came out of the building.

They both saw him at the same moment. Krause stepped

out of the doorway, a cigarette in one hand, and he took a drag on the cigarette and flipped it toward the curb. He was wearing a tan trench coat, unbelted, the cloth belt flapping. His shoes were highly polished. He moved toward the curb, and Jill turned the key in the ignition and pulled out of the parking space. The Ford rolled forward. Dave took the gun from her purse and held it just below the window on his side.

There were two cars parked in front of Krause's building with a four-foot space between them. Krause stood at the curb's edge between the two cars. He moved out to cross, saw the Ford, and stepped back to let it pass him. The Ford moved even with Krause. Dave braced the barrel of the gun on the window frame. Jill hit the brake, not too hard, and the car slowed.

Krause looked at them. There was an instant of recognition—of the gun, of Dave. Then Dave emptied the gun at him.

One bullet missed and broke glass in the door of the building. The other four bullets were on target. Three hit Krause in the body, one in the stomach and two in the center of the chest. The final bullet caught him as he was falling and took half his head off. The combined force of the shots lifted Dago Krause off his feet and tossed him back on the curb. He never had time to move, never uttered a sound.

Jill's foot left the brake pedal and put the accelerator on the floor. The Ford jumped forward as though startled and raced straight ahead for two blocks. There was a red light at the second intersection. She slowed the car briefly, then took a hard left through the light and sped down that street for two more blocks. She turned again, right this time, and slowed down to normal speed. The .38 was back in her purse, the window rolled up. The car had a heavy gunpowder smell to it, and he opened the vent slightly to let it air out.

On a residential street about a mile away she stopped the car and he got out and switched the plates. The whole operation—removal of the Jersey plates and substitution of his own—took less than five minutes. He got back in the car and she headed for the Triborough Bridge again while he wiped his fingerprints from the stolen license plates. When they passed a vacant lot, she slowed the car and he unrolled the window and threw the plates out into the middle of the field.

They crossed the bridge. She drove the width of Manhattan on 125th Street, then stopped at the entrance to the Henry Hudson Parkway and let him take the wheel. He headed north on the Henry Hudson, picked up the Saw Mill River Parkway and followed the throughway signs. There were three bridges to cross and a lot of tolls to pay, and the traffic was moderately heavy on the Saw Mill River Parkway, but they were on the throughway by noon.

# *18*

<<<<<<<<<<<<<<<<<<<<<<<<<<<<<<<<<<<<<<<<<<<<<<<<<<<

THE SKY was turning dark. They stood together at the crest of the hill and looked out over the rolling countryside. There was very little traffic on the highway. The sun had set minutes ago. There was a red glow to the west. Behind them, the motel's neon sign winked on and off, on and off.

The motel was on Route 28, a two-lane state highway that curved through the Catskills. They had left the throughway at the Saugerties exit and had driven this far before he decided to call it a day. They spent the afternoon by the side of the motel pool, ate dinner at a roadhouse a few miles down the road to the east.

She said, "I can't believe it, you know."

"That it's over?"

"That it's over. Or that it happened at all, the crime or the punishment. Neither one seems real now. Just eight days, I can't believe any of it."

He slipped an arm around her waist. She leaned against him and he smelled the fragrance of her hair. "After a year," she said, "we won't be able to believe it at all, any of it. You'll be a very very promising young attorney and I'll be a charming young married in the social swim and it will seem so completely unreal we'll think we dreamed it."

He kissed her. She looked at him with the biggest eyes on earth and he held her close and kissed her again, and when he released her there was no need to say anything, not a word. Together they turned and walked to their room. The door was not locked. They went inside, and he locked the door while she drew the blinds. Together, they took the spread off the bed and drew the covers down.

They undressed slowly and silently. He took her in his arms and kissed her again, gently, and she sighed, and he drew her down upon the bed and lay down beside her. She was incredibly beautiful.

"My wife," he whispered. "My love."

There were tears in the corners of her eyes. She blinked them away. His hands filled up with the warmth of her body, and desire welled up within him, a living force. He had never wanted anything, ever, as much as he wanted her now.

The bars were gone, the blocks were kicked aside. When it was time, her thighs opened to him and her breasts cushioned him. He took her, and she gave a small sweet cry of joy, and they were together.

Whole concepts fled—time, space, memory, self. Love

lived its own life, an island to itself, and sleep came quick on its heels.

They spent four days at the motel. Almost all of that time was spent in the room, in the bed. Their need for each other was overpowering, irresistible. They would laugh about it and tell each other that they had turned into sex maniacs, and suddenly the laughter and the banter would die in the air and they would fall hungrily back into bed.

Once she said, "I'm very good, aren't I?"

"And modest too."

"But good," she said, yawning. "Am I the best you ever had?"

"The only one I ever had."

"Ah." She yawned again, stretching her arms high overhead. "But I don't mind the others," she said. "I'm not even a little jealous. They couldn't make you like this. Only me."

And another time, after a meeting that was fast and furious, she put her head on his chest and cried. He stroked her hair and asked her what was the matter. She wouldn't tell him. He held her in silence, and after a few minutes she looked up at him with tears in her eyes, tears staining her cheeks.

She said, "I wish—"

"What?"

"That I could have been a virgin for you."

"But you were," he said.

She thought that over for a few minutes. Then, slowly, she nodded. "Yes," she said, "I was, wasn't I?"